The GHOSTS of WESTTHORPE ACADEMY

D1073833

JOSEPH LEWIS

ELECTIO PUBLISHING
first century principles.
a twenty-first century approach.

The Ghosts of Westthorpe Academy
By Joseph Lewis

Copyright 2018 by Joseph Lewis. All rights reserved.
Cover Design by eLectio Publishing

ISBN-13: 978-1-63213-520-9

Published by eLectio Publishing, LLC

Little Elm, Texas

http://www.eLectioPublishing.com

5 4 3 2 1 eLP 22 21 20 19 18

Printed in the United States of America.

The eLectio Publishing creative team is comprised of: Kaitlyn Campbell, Emily Certain, Lori Draft, Jim Eccles, Sheldon James, and Christine LePorte.

Publisher's Note

The publisher does not have any control over and does not assume any responsibility for author or third-party websites or their content.

To Fr. Gerry,
Thank you so much for important advice, prayers, and technical assistance in helping make this book possible. Please accept this as a token of my appreciation. God bless you.

To my wife Marian who has always encouraged me to write. Thank you for your abiding love and support.

All the best,
Joe Lewis

Acknowledgments

A SPECIAL THANKS to Father Gerry Olinger, CSC, and Laura Mondon, whose technical advice and generous assistance were essential in making this book possible.

To my brother John, a writer and published author himself, who has always been an inspiration to me.

To the members of my family, especially those who volunteered to read through the early editions of the book. Your editorial assistance, creative contributions, suggestions, and honest opinions (though painful at times) went a long way in helping bring the book to completion. I could not have done it without you.

Finally, I would like to thank all the students, faculty, staff, and families who I have had the privilege of knowing over the years at Devon Preparatory School (a school very much like Westthorpe Academy). This book is in many ways a tribute to all of you. Thank you for allowing me to be a part of your lives. *Laudetur Jesus Christus, In aeternum, Amen!*

May the Lord bless you all, and Mary keep you.

Chapter 1

AS THE FAMILY VAN pulled up to the front of the school, he noticed immediately the large and impressive stone mansion that stood before them. His parents were bringing him to Westthorpe Academy for a visit. Having just graduated from eighth grade at Saint Philomena's, he had told his parents he preferred going to the high school most of his friends would be attending—Pope Benedict XVI High School, which was not far from where they lived.

But because two of his uncles on his mother's side had attended Westthorpe, and his younger cousin was surely destined to go there, his parents had persuaded him to "at least take a look at it." They liked the fact that the school had a reputation for high academic standards and placed a strong emphasis on good religious instruction in the Catholic faith.

He and his parents got out of the van and began walking across the school lawn. It was a beautiful late-spring day with a scattering of low hanging clouds against a blue sky as a gentle breeze swept through the green leaves of the surrounding trees. As they moved closer to the mansion, the building's features became more distinct. It was constructed of grayish-colored stone with what looked like gargoyles perched high atop two triangular points where the front walls met the red-tiled roof. Rising from the center back of the building was a large, fortress-like, block-shaped tower that offered what appeared to be a very favorable view above the roof. It was complete with a parapet at the very top with small rectangular indentations on all four sides which gave it a certain medieval look. Perfect, he imagined, for the launching of arrows or other such projectiles should the castle come under attack by an invading enemy. At the very least, he thought, the school buildings did have a certain charm about them.

Upon entering through the large front entrance, they were greeted at the door by a handsomely dressed gentleman with a bright smile on his face. "Hello, Pryce family," he said, as he extended his hand toward Mr. Pryce. "I'm Jack Ritter, Director of Admissions. Welcome to Westthorpe Academy!" After also shaking hands with Mrs. Pryce, he then turned and said, "And you must be George!" Now the name George was certainly correct, and was the name given to him at birth, and, no doubt, was written in the appropriate margin on the school application. However, it was not a name he had necessarily used as he grew up, and his family seemed perfectly willing to allow an alternative first name to eventually come about. This was due in no small part to his younger sister Kate, short for Katharine, named after Saint Katharine Drexel. George's middle name was Owen. The names George and Owen were both borrowed from relatives, one from each side of the family. As George grew up, his mother often referred to him as George Owen when calling out his name. His little sister could never quite get the combination right, and it would often come out as "Jo-Jo." Well, it didn't take long for that to simply become "Joe" or "Joey" as he got older. This very much pleased his grandmother on his mother's side, whose husband, and his grandfather, Joe, short for Joseph, had passed away a number of years ago. In fact, it pleased her so much that Grandma actually started calling him Joseph, which was okay too.

"Nice to meet you, Mr. Ritter. They call me Joe," he said as he shook Mr. Ritter's hand.

"Great to meet you too, Joe," he said. Mr. Ritter then escorted them into the main hall of the building. "We are currently in what was the original building of the school when it first opened. This is the manor house or mansion that was once part of the estate known as Westthorpe Farm which was owned by the Wallingford family. The Wallingfords were, at one time, one of the most prominent families in the Philadelphia area." Mr. Ritter then pointed toward a large fireplace within the great hall covered by an ornately decorated mantel. "In fact, if you look closely just above the fireplace, inscribed within the mantel is the date the mansion was completed, '1914,' and the original name of the property, 'Westthorpe.'" As someone who enjoyed learning about history, Joe looked up and read the inscription with a curious fascination. "This building," continued Mr. Ritter, "is now called Moreau Hall, named after Blessed Father Basil Moreau, the founder of the Congregation of Holy Cross. The order bought this property in the late 1940s and opened the school a short time later. Moreau Hall is now almost exclusively where the administrative offices are located and where the residences of the priests of the order who teach here are located, on the upper floor."

Mr. Ritter had the kind of personality suited for his job—extroverted and quite the conversationalist. Although Joe had never formally met Mr. Ritter before, he had seen him on local ballfields coaching older soccer and baseball players in athletic leagues where he also played. Aside from his administrative duties, Mr. Ritter coached both sports at the school, so Joe immediately felt like there was something the two of them could relate to. Before he knew it, they were talking about next fall's soccer season at Westthorpe and how, with so many senior players having graduated this past year, there would be a number of opportunities for newer guys coming into the program.

Westthorpe Academy was situated just west of Philadelphia, Pennsylvania, along the famous "Main Line," a suburban region known for its elite social status and "old money." Though the school hardly considered itself as having much to do with either of those descriptions, it had certainly developed a fine reputation for strong academics and competitive sports, and it enjoyed the support of the surrounding community. As Mr. Ritter explained, the school had been started by the Congregation of Holy Cross almost seventy years ago, the same order that runs the University of Notre Dame as well as a number of other schools and colleges throughout the country and the world. In recent years, however, due mostly to the limited number of vocations, the order could no longer continue to staff enough priests and brothers to oversee the running of the school. Fortunately, a dedicated group of alumni and families got together and proposed a plan to keep the school going with an increased emphasis on lay people helping staff and run the school. It was approved by the provincial superior of Holy Cross, with the congregation continuing to sponsor the school.

The headmaster was now a lay person as were most of the faculty. A couple of the priests from the order who were semi-retired still remained and were part-time teachers which the school was happy to have. Westthorpe Academy remained rooted in many of the fine traditions of the order although much of its authority in overseeing the running of the school was now shared within the board of trustees.

~~~~~

The following Saturday morning, Joe took the entrance exam at Westthorpe and then had to hurry to be able to catch the first inning of his Babe Ruth League baseball game at noon. He was an intelligent student but was not likely to be getting a full scholarship to go to Westthorpe. His parents told him not to worry about that and that they would simply see how he did on the exam and decide from there. Although he reminded them that tuition at Pope Benedict would be considerably less, they insisted that

Westthorpe was still a strong contender as far as they were concerned.

Joe's family was far from wealthy, and both his mom and dad had made many sacrifices in raising their five children. Joe, fourteen, was the oldest followed by Kate, who was thirteen, and then twin sisters Anna and Therese (whom everyone called Tess), who were both nine, and little brother Bobby, who was five. Mom had shared with them that after having had a miscarriage a couple of years ago, she had been told that she would probably not be able to have more children. She was accepting of this, having always taught her children that God had a purpose in all things. She felt blessed to have the children she had and was committed to loving the ones that God had given her.

As much as the thought of going to Westthorpe had, admittedly, begun to grow on him, Joe was more than happy at the prospect of attending Pope Benedict. There, he could be with his friends, still get a get a good education, and, yes, talk to girls, something Westthorpe severely lacked. He felt there were advantages with each of the schools and that he would be fine going to either one.

~~~~~

The summer was well underway, and Joe had already decided to continue his lawn cutting business, which had done pretty well the previous year. He had always helped his dad cut their own lawn, and by the time he was old enough, it had become one of his primary chores. His parents had always expected him and his siblings to be of help around the house. Joe enjoyed manual work and particularly liked being outside. To him, there was nothing like the sights, sounds, and smells of the great outdoors. He loved camping (which his family did every summer) and hitting the trails, whether hiking or on his mountain bike. The money he made last year from his lawn service allowed him to purchase his bike, which he desperately needed to get into the bike shop for a much-needed tune-up before getting back on the trails this summer.

Although he was now of age to get a work permit, being fourteen still had its restrictions on the number and type of hours he could work at a restaurant or any other place of business. And because he had been successful in getting a good many neighbors as regular customers for his lawn service, he decided he would do that again this year. Furthermore, Kate was driving him crazy about wanting to be a "partner," as she called it. Late last summer, she had expressed an interest in helping out, which he was glad to accept—at least he thought so at the time. Joe soon discovered that as much as she was of help with doing some of the cutting around the edges where the larger mower couldn't go or trimming back some hedges, she was always trying to make suggestions about how the work could be done better. To be honest, he did appreciate her help, but was he willing to put up with the persistent faultfinding that came with it?

Somehow, they managed to make it through last year's grass cutting season without too much incident. However, this year, Kate let it be known that she was not satisfied with being paid by the hour, although Joe reminded her he was paying her well above minimum wage—and tax free! She replied that she had been responsible for bringing in new customers (maybe one as he remembered it), and as such, should be getting a share of the business.

It wasn't long before such discussions spilled over into the family dinner hour, and eventually Mom and Dad informed them that they would have to work things out between themselves. Actually, he and Kate normally got along pretty well. They were close in age and shared in a lot of common interests like sports, playing the piano, reading, going to the movies, playing cards, and altar serving at church. In fact, Mom and Dad were always amazed at how close they were, which is why they were a bit surprised by the recent squabble.

Fortunately, cooler heads soon prevailed. Kate informed Joe that she was probably going to have to cut back on helping out anyway with all she was doing that summer. They were both going on service trips to the Appalachia in July, though Kate's trip was different from Joe's and would be a week longer than his. Furthermore, she was taking a math course over the summer as well. With this in mind, Joe proposed that he would be willing to increase her wage, which she was satisfied with. This was probably what she wanted all along, he thought. Regardless, everything was resolved between the two of them, peace was restored, and everybody was happy!

~~~~~

The following week, Joe rushed home after cutting one too many lawns on a warm and muggy June afternoon. No doubt, he thought, this was the beginning of a stretch of hot, humid weather that was typical of southeastern Pennsylvania during this time of the year. As he approached the house, Joe's mom was waiting for him at the front door. "I know, I'm sorry. I'm not supposed to come through the front door with my work boots on," he said as he brushed past her, fully expecting to get scolded. "I'm in a hurry to get to my baseball game at 5:30, and I need to put my uniform in the dryer," he continued as he struggled to untie his boots.

"Joe dear," she said rather calmly, "you'll find your uniform neatly folded on your bed."

"Thanks, Mom—you're the best," he said as he kissed her on the cheek.

"But before you go running off," she told him, "I want you to see this." She handed him an envelope. "I realize it's addressed to you, but I knew you wouldn't mind if I opened it. It's from Westthorpe Academy." As he removed the piece of paper inside and began to open it, she was not about to wait for him to discover for himself before she divulged its contents. "You did well enough on the entrance exam that they are offering you a scholarship that will cover half tuition!"

Joe began to look more intently at the letter, signed by Mr. Ritter, confirming what his mom had just said. "I have no doubt," she continued, "that your dad would agree with me that this will put both tuitions very much the same." For Joe, this was a complete surprise. He never seriously thought Westthorpe would work out and had already begun making plans to attend Pope Benedict in the fall. In fact, he was fully prepared to participate in the school's informal summer practices for soccer during the coming weeks. And besides, his friends fully expected him to be at Benedict with them.

"Wait a minute, Mom," he announced. "Let's not get carried away. There are other things to think about too."

"Such as?" she quickly responded.

"Well, Benedict is practically down the street—I can almost walk there! Westthorpe is a lot further, and somebody would have to drive me there every day!"

"That shouldn't be an issue," she assured him. "I know they have a bus that comes out this way."

"But if I'm doing soccer or baseball or something after school, getting home is gonna be a problem."

"Look," she replied, "whether you realize it or not, your dad and I have talked about this very possibility and have already addressed these concerns. We both agree we can make things work out."

By this time, Joe began to realize he had to clean up, get dressed, grab a quick bite to eat from the kitchen, and get to his game. "Why don't we talk about this later, Mom? I really need to get going."

"Of course, dear. We all plan on coming to the game after your dad gets home."

"You really don't have to," replied Joe. "We're playing Marshfield, and I don't think it's going to be pretty. They beat us pretty badly last time," he said as he bounded up the steps to get ready to go.

~~~~~

"Cheese and crackers!" his coach said as he threw the gum that was in his mouth to the concrete floor of the dugout in disgust. The game ended abruptly with a bottom of the seventh inning walk-off home run by the clean-up hitter for Marshfield on a hanging curveball from Charlie Barto. By this time in the game, Joe was sitting next to his coach after having pitched the previous two innings in relief while keeping the game close. His team had come back from behind to tie the game in the top of the seventh only to have it end this way. "Cheese and crackers!" he blurted out again, "I knew we shouldn't have pitched to that guy!"

Though the game had ended in defeat, Joe couldn't help but chuckle a little at the way his coach, Ned Campbell, had been working hard to live up to his self-imposed commitment to cutting back on his swearing and other "colorful" expressions. Though he was careful not to use some of them within earshot of parents and younger siblings who came to the games, Joe and the rest of the players had, on occasion, heard them in the dugout and on the field, especially considering the way the team had been playing of late. In place of some of those expressions, he would substitute words that were certainly more acceptable for public consumption but sounded a lot like what he was trying to avoid saying. And as much as they had to give Coach credit for trying, there was obviously still room for improvement.

Aside from his little idiosyncrasies, they all liked Coach Campbell and wished they could play better for him, if only to help him with his swearing. He was definitely "old school," loved baseball, and enjoyed coaching. He had played semi-pro ball a number of years ago but had to give it up due to a nagging back injury, and with it, his dream of playing in the big leagues. During his playing days, he had affectionately been nicknamed "Soup," not surprising given his last name, but the players knew they could never call him that.

"Dagnabbit!" as he turned to Mr. Figueroa, one of the dads who helped keep score and coach the team. "The way that guy hits, we should've given him first base and pitched to the next guy," he said in frustration.

"That would have put the winning run on first with no outs," replied Mr. Figueroa. "Not so sure you want to do that, Coach. Can't second guess yourself. We lost to a good team, and our guys played well. They never gave up and kept coming back. Don't beat yourself up."

"You're right, Pete," he replied with some resignation, "I gotta give 'em that."

As the team walked slowly and dejectedly off the field, the players on other side of the diamond were celebrating the jubilation of another victory. Joe went out to meet the pitcher, Charlie Barto. "Forget about it, Chuck. That guy's a tough out. Besides, you played a heck of a game with a dinger of your own that tied it up and gave us a chance to win."

"Thanks, man," he said softly but continued toward the dugout with his head down. This was definitely a tough one for everyone to swallow.

After the game, Coach Campbell was surprisingly calm and told them how proud he was of the way they kept fighting and didn't quit. He told them to keep their heads high and not let anything get them down. No doubt Mr. Figueroa's consolatory and softer approach had a positive influence on Coach.

After the talk, Joe grabbed his bat bag and headed out of the dugout. As he walked toward the stands, he was immediately jumped on by his twin sisters.

"Hey Joe, we thought you played great!" said Tess.

"Yeah," followed Anna, "Dad said they should've left you in the game."

"I don't know about that," he responded.

"Can I carry your bag?" asked Bobby as he tried to pull it off Joe's shoulder.

"I don't know, little man, it's still a little heavy for you," he told him. "Where's Kate?"

"She's spending the night at a friend's house," said Anna.

"Someone from her soccer team I think," said Tess.

"Yeah, and they're sleeping out in a tent," said Anna.

As twins who were rarely ever apart, they were always starting and finishing sentences together. It was actually kind of cute.

"That sounds like fun," remarked Joe.

As they made their way to the parking lot, Mom was talking to Mrs. Figueroa while Dad came over to greet him. "We're proud of you, sonny boy," said his dad as he used one arm to pick up Bobby while reaching out with the other to place a hand on Joe's shoulder. "I must admit, though, I do think they should've left you in the game."

"So the girls told me," responded Joe, "but I wasn't really surprised, knowing how Coach Campbell likes to use Charlie late in games like that—with his kind of stuff."

"I don't know," replied his dad, "those Marshfield hitters sure like sitting on the fastball, and that's probably Charlie's best pitch." Dad played some ball in high school back in the day and enjoyed a stint of coaching Joe in his earlier Little League years. He was always very supportive and not one to criticize, but if he felt something needed to be said, he would say his piece and then that would be the end of it. He always encouraged the kids not to dwell on the things they couldn't change, but rather focus on the things ahead of them.

Having ridden his bike to the game, Joe was happy to have a ride home. As he positioned the bike on the rack on the back of the minivan, up ran Pete Figueroa Jr., or "Fig" as he was often referred to, especially on the ballfield. "You played a heck of a game, Fig. What did you have, three hits?" asked Joe.

"Just two, with a walk," he responded. "Listen," he continued, "what's this I hear you still might be going to Westthorpe?"

That didn't take long, Joe thought to himself as he remembered seeing his mom talking with Mrs. Figueroa. "Look," said Joe, "I've said from the beginning that as much as my parents seem to like the idea, I still don't see any way that's going to happen. Besides, we've got to keep the group together, right?" asked Joe.

"I'm just telling you, my friend," remarked Fig, "that's not how I'm hearing it. We're gonna miss you over at Pope Benedict. I gotta run. See you at the concert this weekend."

"Ready dear?" called Joe's mom from the passenger side window. "Dad has promised to take us out for ice cream!"

"I'm coming, I'm coming!" exclaimed Joe as he climbed into the back of the van. Nothing like ice cream to help you forget about having lost the game.

"Where should we go, Handel's or Maggie Moo's?" asked Mom.

"Why don't we do Maggie Moo's," suggested Joe.

"You just want to see that pretty girl, Evelyn, who works there," replied Anna.

"Handel's is better," protested Tess. "Let's go there!"

"Maggie Moo's is closer, and besides, you can't beat their Red Velvet Cake ice cream," responded Dad.

"I agree," said Mom, and the decision was made.

"Can we get double scoops?" asked Tess.

"And extra toppings?" followed Anna.

Chapter 2

THE BELL RANG, and Joe was in his assigned seat in homeroom, ready for the first day of school. Pete Figueroa was right next to him, one row over, as the alphabetized seating arrangement placed them. "Welcome to homeroom, gentlemen," announced Mr. McAuliffe. "These are your assigned seats and will remain that way throughout the year." Okay, thought Joe, at least he wasn't at the very front.

As Mr. McAuliffe was finishing up going over a few things, a second bell rang, and a deep male voice was suddenly on the school intercom inviting everyone to stand.

"This is your fault," whispered Pete to Joe.

"You gotta be quiet," Joe whispered back to Pete.

"That's enough, gentlemen," Mr. McAuliffe said and signaled to both of them. "We're about to pray."

"Good morning, Westthorpe Academy! Please stand for our morning prayer. In the name of the Father, and the Son, and the

Holy Spirit, Amen," the voice continued. "Come, O Holy Spirit, fill the hearts of your faithful and enkindle in them the fire of your love; send forth your spirit, and they shall be created, and You shall renew the face of the earth. Let us pray. O God, who, by the light of the Holy Spirit, instructed the faithful, grant that by the same Holy Spirit we may be truly wise and rejoice in His consolation, through Christ Our Lord. Amen."

He then concluded with, "May God bless you all and grant success to the work of your hands, in the name of the Father, and the Son, and the Holy Spirit, Amen. Remember, gentlemen, you are the living image of Christ. May all your actions today be for his greater glory and the good of your neighbor." After a brief pause, the voice of a student then immediately followed with, "*Ad Dei Gloriam,*" which Joe knew, even with the little Latin he had studied, meant "For the glory of God."

The same voice then led everyone in the Pledge of Allegiance, followed by a few announcements, and finished with an exuberant "Knights of Westthorpe—*Semper Invicta!*"

As a veteran teacher at Westthorpe, Mr. McAuliffe always enjoyed teaching the freshmen. They were like sponges, soaking up everything you threw at them, enthusiastic about learning, motivated, and eager to please. But he also knew that some of them could be painfully shy when it came to raising their hand to ask a question, especially on the first day of school. Knowing he had an extended homeroom that morning, he wanted to take the opportunity to explain to the students what they had just heard during the announcements. He invited them to sit back down in their seats.

"Gentlemen, that was the traditional rallying cry of our school. When the school first opened many years ago, it adopted 'Knights' as the school nickname. This was done to honor the men of religious orders of the Middle Ages that were formed to help protect pilgrims and other travelers who visited the Holy Land in Palestine. They were monks who took the traditional vows of poverty, chastity, and obedience and dedicated themselves to a life of prayer, piety, and a willingness to risk their own lives in the defense of others. This was the expectation of every monk—that they would conduct themselves bravely and nobly, not only in battle, but in everything they did. And the same characteristics often associated with a knight, such as chivalry, fortitude, resilience, piety, and scholarship are very much a part of what our school is all about and tries to instill in each of its students."

Mr. McAuliffe would go on to explain that one of the great saints and doctors of the Church, Saint Bernard of Clairvaux, had helped the pope of that time inspire and organize the Second Crusade, sending many knights to help restore and defend the Holy Land in the twelfth century. "And as much as St. Bernard must have been a dog lover," suggested Mr. McAuliffe, "having expressed the saying 'Love me, love my dog' in one of his homilies centuries ago, he is not the same saint for whom the dog is named after!"

"Really, Mr. McAuliffe?" asked one of the students, whom Joe was not yet familiar with, from the back of the classroom. "Then where do we get the name from?"

"Very good question," responded Mr. McAuliffe. "That honor goes to Saint Bernard of *Menthon* who actually lived a hundred years earlier."

After a brief pause to allow his students to absorb all he was sharing with them, he suddenly took a slight detour and made a concession that they would soon discover was quite out of character for Mr. McAuliffe. "Now gentlemen," he remarked, "who am I to allow historical facts to stand in the way of fine traditions? Here, at Westthorpe Academy, for example, our mascot is a St. Bernard dog, though it has little to do with the knights of the Middle Ages. But as long as I can remember, and I've been here a long time, there has always been a St. Bernard dog connected with the school. One of our retired priests, Father Gusztav, owns the most recent one, named Bernie of course. I'm sure you'll have a chance to see him around campus and at Westthorpe sporting events. If you haven't done so already, take the opportunity to visit the statue of one of the earlier Bernies that stands in the front lawn of the school. Patting his head is strongly encouraged for good luck."

"Yeah, I've done that already," exclaimed a student.

"Me too," said another.

"Now, the Latin expression *'Semper Invicta,'*" continued Mr. McAuliffe, "when translated into English, means 'always invincible,' or 'forever unconquered.' It originated here at Westthorpe a number of years ago when Father Sarjinski, whom some of you may have already met, and whose voice you just heard leading us in prayer, helped coach the baseball team. He would use the phrase to inspire the team to victory on the ballfield. Being of Polish descent, he borrowed the expression from the motto of the city of Warsaw, the capital of Poland, where much of his family is from originally."

Suddenly, Mr. McAuliffe stopped and looked at the clock on the wall above the door. "All right, gentlemen, you've got about two minutes until the bell rings for you to go to your first-period class."

Pete reached over and touched Joe's arm. "I'm not so sure I'm ready for this," he said, rather worriedly.

"Relax," responded Joe, "everything's going to be fine. You've gotta give it a chance. Besides, have you seen the school calendar? We've definitely got longer Christmas and Easter breaks than B-16."

"B-16, what's that?" asked another student sitting on the other side of Joe.

"B-16. You know, Pope Benedict XVI High School," said Joe.

"Oh yeah," said the student.

"By the way, I'm Joe Pryce," he said as he extended a hand.

"Vince Hamden," he responded as he shook Joe's hand.

"Vince, this is Pete, Pete Figueroa."

"How are ya?" said Pete as they also shook hands.

"Where ya from, Vince?" asked Joe.

"I'm from the city," he said.

"What school did you go to last year?" followed Joe.

"I went to Central Middle," answered Vince.

"Wow," said Joe, "that's quite a commute for you, isn't it?"

"I take the train and then get picked up from the station by the school van," he said. "It's not too bad."

Suddenly, the bell was ringing, and everybody was moving. "Off to first period," said Joe.

"What do you have?" asked Vince.

"Geometry," he answered, "in room . . ." He paused to look down at his schedule. "Room 301. How about you?"

"Algebra II, room 210. I think they're both in St. Joseph's Hall."

"Sounds great. Let's go," said Joe. "Come on, Pete. We're gonna be late."

"I'm comin'," he said. "Besides, what's your rush? The worst they can do is throw us out of school, right?"

"Don't get any bright ideas," said Joe.

As they made their way to their classes, Joe couldn't help thinking about his friend, Pete. When it was finally settled that Joe was going to Westthorpe, Pete's parents, who had been mulling it over themselves, unbeknownst to practically everyone, finally decided they wanted him to attend as well. As much as Joe was prepared in advance, this was a surprise for Pete, who had already placed a Pope Benedict sticker on the family car window.

"I think we've got history together sixth period," said Joe to Pete. "I'll see you then. It's gonna be okay, right pal?"

"Of course," said Pete, somewhat less than enthusiastic. "But lunch is right before that—best period of the day!"

"That's the spirit!" responded Joe. "That's the Pete I know. I'll see ya later."

~~~~~

"That's heresy!" declared Father Al Sarjinski with his deep, commanding voice as he answered a rather silly question asked by one of the students in Joe's theology class. Joe quickly discovered, along with everyone else, that it was not difficult to get a rise out of Father Al (short for Alfons). Father Sarjinski was sometimes referred to simply as "Sarge," done so affectionately, mostly by upperclassmen. Father was of medium build with a rather wide girth, wore glasses, and had thinning grayish-brown hair. He had been with the school for a good part of his priesthood and was semi-retired, but he still taught a couple of theology classes, helped moderate the school newspaper, and served as the school chaplain. In years past, he had actually taught math at the University of Notre Dame. "What were they teaching you in eighth grade, Mr. Schumacher?" asked Father. "Whatever it was, we need to straighten it out." A spattering of laughter followed from the class, including from Danny Schumacher himself. "All right, gentlemen," responded Father, "let's get back to the lesson."

As Joe would come to find out, as much as Father Al could be entertaining, he was extremely intelligent, a fine priest, and someone you could talk to. Joe would find this a great comfort, especially when there was confession available in the school chapel, and Father Al was there to go to.

The bell rang, marking not only the end of class but the end of the school day. All in all, things had gone well enough for the first day of school. It was now time to get to soccer practice. "Hey, Pete," Joe called out as he hustled down the hall and saw his friend. "Ready for soccer?"

"I don't know," replied Pete.

"Whad'ya mean, you don't know?" asked Joe.

"Well, I gotta tell ya, during gym today, Mr. Warwick invited me to come out for cross-country. We did some running on the track today, and he thinks I could be good."

As Joe listened, a part of him was happy to know Pete was feeling wanted at their new school. Besides, Pete was always better at baseball than he was at soccer, and when he gets on base, he can run from first to third faster than most. "Have you talked to Coach Ritter?" asked Joe.

"Not yet," said Pete, "but I think I might tell him now before the start of practice."

"I'll go with ya," said Joe.

"I really like Mr. Warwick," offered Pete as they made their way down to the locker room. "He's the coolest guy. Do you know he was in Naval Intelligence and later worked for the CIA? He really got into some of the stories about Moreau Hall today. He's a graduate of Westthorpe and was telling us how, when he was a student here, all the priests who taught at the school and lived in the upper floor of the mansion used to talk about how the place was haunted!"

"Really," responded Joe, sounding rather unconvinced.

"The story goes that a woman named Madame Duchesne used to live in the mansion. According to Mr. Warwick, she was a widow and the mother of a daughter who was a French debutante. The daughter married a wealthy American named James Wallingford."

"Uh-huh," responded Joe.

"After Madame Duchesne's husband died, she came to live here with her daughter and son-in-law. She really missed her husband and spent most of her time tending to the garden. One day, she died suddenly right here in the mansion, from a broken heart, or so they say."

"A rather sad story," said Joe.

"Anyway," Pete went on, "over the years, people claim to have heard voices or seen strange things happen in the mansion. Some are convinced it's Madame Duchesne walking the halls, maybe in search of her husband." Joe gave a look suggesting he wasn't quite convinced himself. "Ask Father Al if you don't believe me," countered Pete, "he'll tell you. He lives in the upper residence of the mansion, so he has a few stories of his own to tell, according to Mr. Warwick."

"Maybe I'll ask Father about it in class tomorrow so we can all have a good laugh," said Joe, snickering a bit.

"Yeah, I knew you'd probably react that way," responded Pete.

They entered the breezeway next to the gym that led to the locker room and Coach Ritter's office. "I'm gonna pop in and talk to Coach. I'll let you know how it goes," said Pete.

"I'll be in the locker room. Good luck."

~~~~

Every first Friday of the month, the Holy Sacrifice of the Mass was offered at Westthorpe in the school's auditorium. Mass was also offered in the school's chapel, named in honor of Our Lady of Consolation, every morning before school began. A fair number of students and faculty were usually able to attend the daily Mass. Joe tried to get there when he could, but it all depended on when he was able to arrive at school each morning. When he did go, sometimes his dad had time enough himself to go with him. "No better way to start the day," his dad often said.

On this particular first Friday, Joe had been asked by Fr. Al if he could fill in as an altar server for another student who was absent that day. Not long after his graduation from St. Philomena's, Joe had decided to suspend his altar serving days after having done it for as long as he could remember while attending school and going to Mass there. However, Fr. Al had approached him during the first week of the new school year to consider joining the school ministry club that helped set up for Mass and orchestrated the monthly Living Rosary and a number of other liturgical functions, which Joe was happy to do. Today, Father needed him to help serve Mass, and suddenly Joe found himself in the sacristy of the school chapel, trying to find the right sized alb to wear for Mass.

"Good morning, Joe," said Father Al, suddenly appearing from the other side of the door that led to the sanctuary of the chapel. "Thank you for helping this morning."

"Not a problem, Father," replied Joe as he fumbled with the alb he was trying on.

"Well, that will never do!" protested Father as he looked down and saw that Joe's alb was far too short. Joe was tall and lean, too lean, he always thought. He kept trying to put on more weight but wasn't having much success. His mom would always tell him to enjoy it while he could.

"You need something that reaches somewhere near the top of your shoes," suggested Father. "Did you happen to know the use of the alb goes back many years in liturgical worship?"

By now, Joe was very accustomed to Father Al's penchant for anecdotes and storytelling. They were always told in such a way that was interesting and taught you something you didn't know before. "In the traditions of ordination in the Church," Father continued, "the acolyte, one who assisted the priest on the altar, like today's altar server, was one of four minor orders eventually leading up to the priesthood—still practiced in some parts of the Church today. The white linen of the alb symbolizes the self-denial and practice of chastity befitting a priest, worn to the ankles to remind him that he is bound to practice good works throughout his life."

Joe had found a longer alb and was trying it on.

"Much better," exclaimed Father, "and don't forget your cincture," he added as he passed him the ropelike belt worn around the waist of the alb. For Joe, serving on the altar was always something his parents encouraged him to do. But he soon realized that he was doing something very special and that it was a privilege to be invited to be in the sanctuary during the celebration of Mass. "Joe, you do realize why I tell you all these things and ask you to help out with the school ministry?" asked Father. "It's because I think you would make a fine priest."

Somewhat surprised, Joe responded, "Thank you, Father. It's nice of you to say, but I don't know, that's quite a decision to make."

"There's no rush, my friend," said Father. "There's plenty of time to discern such things. We'll have to put it to prayer and ask for the wisdom of the Holy Spirit to help lead you in whatever direction the Lord is calling."

"On that, we can agree," responded Joe.

"Speaking of prayer, it's time for Mass, so we better get started," said Father as he looked at his watch. As Joe bowed his head, Father began the pre-Mass prayer: "*In nomine Patris, et Filii, et Spiritus Sancti, Amen.* O Jesus, by the grace of the heavenly Father and the power of the Holy Spirit, guide us as in all righteousness as we serve You today at the altar so we may always be worthy of Your Presence. Amen."

"Amen," echoed Joe as he blessed himself and then reached up to pull the chord to ring the sacristy bell and announce the beginning of Mass.

Chapter 3

"THE ERA OF GOOD FEELINGS, gentlemen, was the name given to the period between 1817 to 1825, which happened to coincide with the presidency of James Monroe, one of eight presidents from Virginia, the most of any state. Incidentally, four of the first five presidents were from Virginia—Washington, Jefferson, Madison, and Monroe. Now, as I was saying," continued Mr. McAuliffe, "the Era of Good Feelings was given this title by a journalist who noticed that President Monroe was greeted with popular support wherever he traveled throughout the country. However, this was actually somewhat misleading although it is true that the fighting between the different political parties was rather tame during this era—which is more than I can say about our current political climate."

"How does he know all this?" whispered Rick Labella.

"And right out of his head—no notes," added Tim Doolittle.

"Anything you'd like to add to the discussion, Mr. Labella? Or for that matter, Mr. Doolittle?" asked Mr. McAuliffe, noticeably disturbed by the chatter within the classroom during his lecture. "You know, Doolittle, you need to be a little more careful about not be bringing too much attention to yourself, especially considering how your name appropriately describes the limited contribution you have made to our class discussions thus far this quarter." This brought about a couple of laughs from among the students. Mr. McAuliffe was one of the more popular teachers at Westthorpe. He was a graduate of the school and had been a teacher there for over forty years. He was always sharply dressed, usually with a sports jacket or even a suit. His graying hair, which he liked to wear a little long, was always well-groomed. The reason for its length, he explained, was because when he was a student at Westthorpe, he was required to keep his hair very short due to the school regulations of the time. He swore from then on that as soon as he graduated from Westthorpe, he would wear his hair long.

His classroom gave the appearance of something more like a museum and library. Throughout the years, he had collected artifacts, historical documents, rare books, old coins and pictures, as well as a number of the more favored projects done by his students over the years. There were models and replicas of famous places and objects from antiquity such as the Parthenon, Roman battle shields, the Hanging Gardens of Babylon, Egyptian pyramids, and many others. Though Joe had always enjoyed the subject, Mr. McAuliffe's class really made history come alive, making it all the more fascinating to learn!

This was not necessarily the opinion of all of Mr. McAuliffe's students, however. Take Tim Doolittle as an example. Tim already knew he wanted to study electrical engineering in college and was one of the smartest students in the freshman class. He loved science and math, but history was not necessarily one of his favorite subjects. But what drove Mr. McAuliffe absolutely crazy was how Tim was able to put forth a minimal amount of effort compared to other students and still do well enough on Mr. McAuliffe's challenging blue-book tests to maintain an A-minus average in the course. Now, this would have normally been okay with Mr. McAuliffe if it weren't for Tim's penchant for being a distraction in class, which would occasionally lead to getting Mr. McAuliffe's Irish dander up.

But it was always done in a rather playful way and never out of spite or ill will. Mr. McAuliffe would make his point, restore the necessary order in class, all the while cracking a joke, usually directed at a student, and getting everyone to learn something at the same time.

"Yes, sir, Mr. McAuliffe—but what did you say we needed to know for the test tomorrow?" asked Tim.

"Everything, Doolittle!" responded Mr. McAuliffe, rather abruptly. "You already know what to expect! Read the assigned material, study your notes, and out of the fifteen or so topics we have recently discussed, I'll choose four or five of them for you to write about!"

"Thanks, Mr. McAuliffe. Looking forward to it!" replied Tim with a smile on his face. Suddenly, the bell rang, marking the end of class.

"Study hard tonight, gentlemen—and you too, Doolittle! Have a good day, and see you tomorrow!"

~~~~~

As Joe walked down the school hallway, he heard the distinct and comforting voice of Fr. Sarjinski resounding from the lobby. Joe had stayed after school to visit with Dr. Guerrero who taught both his Spanish and Algebra classes. He liked Dr. Guerrero, whom everyone affectionately referred to as "Profe"—short for *profesora* (a female teacher en Espanol). Her classes were challenging but fair, and like most classes at Westthorpe, if you put forth the effort, you usually did well.

"Go ahead, Father, tell us more about the strange occurrences you've experienced in the mansion!" asked Pete Figueroa as he pressed Father Al for another story. This had become a popular custom at Westthorpe, seeing Father Al seated on one of the benches in the school lobby in front of the center office at the end of the school day, holding court with his usual cadre of students who loved to hear his stories or ask his opinion on any number of subjects.

"You've heard pretty much all the ones I'm familiar with," responded Father. "You may want to ask Mr. Warwick. He's got a story or two of his own and is very familiar with the Wallingford family and Madame Duchesne herself. However, I warn you, sometimes you can't tell if Mr. Warwick is merely spinning a yarn and pulling your leg or whether there is any truth to his stories at all. You'll have to figure that out for yourself."

"So this is where I find you," said Joe as he walked up to Pete, who was still anxious to hear more about ghosts in the mansion from Father Al. "This is the guy who said he needed to go over some things with Profe in order to prepare for tomorrow's tests— and then you don't show up!" protested Joe.

"Figueroa, you can't be down here wasting time when you've got work to do," responded Father in agreement.

"I'm not wasting time, Father," argued Pete. "I'm actually considering doing a quarter project for religion class on the history of our school, and you've been giving me some good things to get started with. By the way, Father, do you think you might be available sometime for me to do a videotaped interview with you for the project?"

"As long as you promise me we can talk about more than just ghost stories involving Madame Duchesne," responded Father.

"Absolutely, Father. I really appreciate it. I'll be in touch. I gotta go!"

"Where ya going?" asked Joe.

"You mean, where are *we* going?" retorted Pete. "You've gotta give me everything you and Profe went over. What do ya say we hit the library for a few minutes? Don't worry, we'll stop and get something to eat on the way home—on me!"

Pete was famous for such promises. Too often they would go somewhere, and he would conveniently not have the money to pay, and somebody else would be stuck covering for him. "Just like you paid the last time, and the time before that, right?" Joe reminded him.

"All right, just because you covered for me a couple of times. Not all of us are rich like you, Pryce," remarked Pete.

"Rich?" countered Joe. "What little spending money I do have comes from my summer job. The rest is going toward helping pay for college."

"I think money is overrated anyway," suggested Pete. "Besides, doesn't the Bible say that money is at the root of all evil?"

"Not quite," answered Joe. "It actually says the *love* of money, not money itself. There's a difference."

"Either way, it sure seems to cause a lot of problems in the world," Pete said in reply.

"On that, we can agree," responded Joe. "Wait a minute. Is this your way of preparing me for another sob story about you not having any money for when we stop somewhere on the way home?" But Pete had already picked up his book bag and was saying his goodbyes to Father Al, conveniently ignoring Joe's question.

"You boys study hard now," said Father, "I'll be praying for success on your tests tomorrow."

"Thanks, Father," said Pete. "Come on, Joe. Enough of the foolin' around—we've got work to do!"

"Listen to you," answered Joe as they turned and headed toward the library.

Chapter 4

THE FIRST SEMESTER at Westthorpe had gone by very quickly as Joe was feeling more and more like the school was really becoming his own. He liked the guys in his class, he liked his teachers, and he liked the whole feeling of the place. No school is perfect, of course, but he really felt as if Westthorpe was now an extension of his own family, like a home away from home.

Even though February was the month of his birthday (in which he turned fifteen), Joe was happy to see the beginning of March. The winter was quickly giving over to spring as the little snow that was still left on the school ballfields was gradually melting away. The grass was growing again, and a few early flowers in front of Moreau Hall were beginning to sprout. Baseball tryouts were coming up, and Joe was also thinking about either auditioning for the upcoming musical *Les Miserables* or doing stage crew. There would be a lot going on this spring, and he knew he was going to have to keep up with his studies at the same time.

But this was part of what he liked about Westthorpe. He felt he was being challenged and had to apply himself, and that was as it should be. But he also felt he had good and caring support among his teachers and coaches. People went out of their way to provide you with all the opportunities that Westthorpe had to offer in terms of a student's intellectual, physical, and spiritual development. Joe could honestly say he was happy at Westthorpe, and everything seemed to be going well. With that in mind, Joe could hardly have anticipated the news he was about to receive upon returning home one night after baseball practice.

His mom had his favorite meal, spaghetti and meatballs, waiting in the kitchen. But first, the family would often pray a decade of the rosary before dinner, especially if there was a special intention. His mom was particularly devoted to the rosary and attributed the praying of it to their many blessings. She would always remind the family of the old saying of Father Patrick Peyton that "the family that prays together stays together," as well as "a world at prayer is a world at peace." Father Peyton was famously known as "The Rosary Priest" and had traveled to many parts of the world to promote the praying of the rosary, especially among families. He became somewhat of a media sensation while gaining the admiration and support of many, including a number of Hollywood celebrities.

Mrs. Pryce had closely followed Father Peyton's life. As a graduate herself of Stonehill College in Massachusetts, she was present at his funeral where he was buried in the Holy Cross Cemetery on the grounds of the Stonehill campus. She never grew tired of telling the family how he had been born and raised in Ireland, traveled to the United States and eventually became a priest of the Congregation of Holy Cross. Prior to his ordination, however, it was discovered he had advanced stages of tuberculosis for which nothing could be done. His sister encouraged him to have faith and to rely on the love and intercession of the Blessed

Mother, especially through the praying of the rosary. Not long after, and much to the astonishment of his doctors, the tuberculosis disappeared, and no medical explanation could be offered.

Grateful that his life had been spared, Father Peyton, with the permission of his superiors, devoted his priesthood to bringing devotion to the Blessed Mother through the praying of the Holy Rosary to individuals and families throughout the world. The Catholic Church recently declared him "Venerable," a designation that represents a rare recognition that Father Peyton was a person of heroic virtue who lived a life worthy of veneration. This moved him one step closer to the possibility, God willing, of being fully recognized as a canonized saint of the Church.

"I have a special intention I would like to offer this evening during our rosary," proposed Joe's mom.

"So do I," answered Anna. "Me too," replied Tess, not to be outdone.

"What is it, Mom?" asked Kate with a genuine concern and curiosity.

"I'd rather keep it a silent intention during our prayer and perhaps discuss it sometime later," she replied.

"Very good," said Dad. "Let's get started before supper gets cold."

After the rosary and the saying of grace, everyone settled down to a delicious meal. Mom, however, didn't seem particularly hungry and barely touched her food. After helping clean up, loading the dishwasher, and putting out the garbage, Joe found Mom in the study talking with Dad.

"We're glad you're here, son. Have a seat," Dad said and moved over on the sofa. Mom smiled, but with a look of some concern on her face.

"Something you and Mom want to talk about?" asked Joe.

"Nothing life-threatening or earth-shattering" responded Dad.

"Well, that's a relief," said Joe with a sigh.

"I think your mom can best explain," suggested Dad.

"As you know, Joe," Mom began, "I went to last night's Parents Association meeting for Westthorpe, part of my duties as a member of the committee council. Well, anyway, the meeting was going along fine until one of the parents stood up and said he had heard rumors that the school was having financial difficulties and was considering closing its doors. He wanted to know if this was true."

"Wow!" exclaimed Joe after a brief pause. "This can't be true, is it?"

"Well," answered Dad, "there's no secret that with the economy being down, it's hard to deny that it hasn't had some effect on enrollment—not unlike a number of other private schools like Westthorpe Academy all over the country." As an accountant, Dad always had a way of analyzing things as one looking at a ledger sheet. No doubt he was right, but this was Joe's school they were talking about, a school he had come to love and didn't want to leave.

"What did the administration say when they were asked the question?" Joe wanted to know.

"Headmaster Dr. Nichols seemed somewhat surprised by it," answered Mom. "He hesitated a bit but then basically said you can't believe everything you hear. He explained that, not unlike Dad was suggesting, with the current economy, they would like to see enrollment somewhat higher and their financial status more stable. But he did add that he was confident that things would improve."

"What concerns me," added Mom, "was that none of the other members of the Board of Trustees for the school were there. There are usually at least a couple of them at our meetings."

"Do you really think there's something to this, Mom?" asked Joe.

"I simply don't know sweetheart, but it did seem to concern enough of us at the meeting." She paused for a moment. "I contacted your uncles, Jimmy and Rich, and, as alumni of the school, they are obviously concerned. They told me they would try to make some inquiries with the alumni association to see if anyone has heard anything."

For Joe's mom, Westthorpe Academy had been a part of her life for many years. Her older brothers and Joe's uncles, Jimmy and Rich, had gone to Westthorpe, and she went to St. Rita of Cascia School for Girls during her high school years. St. Rita's wasn't far from Westthorpe and was considered a "sister" school of Westthorpe. The tradition of brothers and sisters within the same family going to both schools had been going on for decades.

"One thing I do want you to do for me," his mom asked, "is not share this with anyone. I would rather we put this to prayer and trust that the Good Lord will take care of everything."

Joe went to bed that night feeling a bit uneasy. Was the school really considering closing? He promised his mother he wouldn't share this concern with anyone else, but he knew he needed to find out. Just the same, though, he couldn't let it bother him. Like Mom suggested, he had to have faith that everything was going to be okay.

~~~~~~~~~

"Let's begin, gentlemen," announced Mr. Gallagher as he entered the bio lab, paused, and began the class with, "*Ave Crux*," which was immediately followed with, "*Spes Unica*," by the students. This Latin motto of the Congregation of Holy Cross was visible in every classroom of the building next to each crucifix and was prayed at the beginning of every class. Mr. Gallagher also used it at the end of each class and asked that it be said in English at that time so as to be reminded of its English translation: "Hail to the Cross, our only hope!"

Today was test day, and although he didn't sleep particularly well the night before, Joe felt confident enough that he was as prepared as he could possibly be. As he received the test, he noticed the familiar "JMJ" at the top of the paper. He paused a moment and said a silent prayer: "Jesus, Mary, and Joseph, please help me and everyone in our class on our test today. Amen."

The period seemed to go very quickly, and he was just able to finish the last question before the bell rang. "How'd ya do, Joe?" asked Larry Turnbull. Larry was a high jumper on the track team, and a pretty good one.

"Hard to say," answered Joe as they left the classroom. "How about you, Leap? Another curve buster for you, I'm sure," he suggested.

Due to his vertical aptitude for jumping over crossbars on the track team and his proficiency for blocking shots and dunking on the basketball court, Larry had affectionately been given the nickname "Leapin' Larry," or just "Leap" for short. In addition to being a fine athlete, he was a pretty darn good student as well. "Not so sure—I think I might have missed one," he answered.

"Yeah, I'll bet," responded Joe.

"Hey, who are you sharing a tent with on the trip?" asked Larry. Every year, each of the classes went on what was referred to as a field studies trip intended to introduce students to educational experiences outside the classroom over the course of several school days. The trips were one of the more popular school events that the students really looked forward to. The freshmen trip involved going to the Gettysburg Battlefield and camping out at one of the nearby campgrounds. On one of the days of the trip, the students were scheduled to go on a guided tour of the battlefield, including a candlelit ghost tour within the town of

Gettysburg in the evening. The trip also included visiting other sites such as attending a baseball game at Camden Yards in Baltimore as well as touring the Inner Harbor and going to nearby Fort McHenry, which inspired the writing of the *Star Spangled Banner* by Francis Scott Key. There was also the opportunity to have some fun at the nearby Sports Emporium complete with laser tag, go-karts, and the latest arcade games.

"It's looking like Fig, Hamden, LaBella, and myself," replied Joe. "How about you, Leap? I'd invite you to be with us, but I don't think you'd fit."

"You're probably right," responded Larry, "and I appreciate that, but I'll be with Brophy and D'Cruze and will have all the space I need."

"It should be fun," said Joe, "as long as it doesn't rain."

"They say you can always count on at least some rain every year," answered Larry. "Either way, it's gonna be a good time! I'll see ya around, Joe. Save me a seat at lunch!"

Chapter 5

JOE HAD DONE EXACTLY as his mother had asked and had not spoken to anyone about what had been discussed at the Parent's Association meeting. Instead, he decided he would keep his eyes and ears open for any signs that might reveal something. He hoped he would not discover anything and simply be able to dismiss the whole thing as an unsubstantiated rumor and nothing more.

As the days went by at school, about the only thing that seemed to be of some concern to Joe involved the sudden change in the business office. For years, Mr. Whitaker had been the business manager at Westthorpe, taught a math class, and coached the JV basketball team. However, it had been no secret that Mr. Whitaker wasn't happy about the way certain things were being conducted by the school of late. What that meant, nobody knew for sure. What did become obvious was the sudden departure of Mr. Whitaker. This was especially difficult given that he was an alum of the school, a former champion rower (when the school had a rowing team), and well-liked by everyone. Apparently, he had been in a recent meeting with Dr. Nichols and a couple of members of the board of trustees, including some visiting priests from the order. The meeting got a little loud, and before you knew it, Mr. Whitaker was announcing his retirement, which he had been threatening to do for some time. He then abruptly got up and left the building.

Saturday evening of that week, Joe returned home from a dance at school and learned from his dad some unsettling news. According to a reliable source, Westthorpe Academy was facing a large payment due on a mortgage loan. The Congregation of Holy Cross order had owned some land across the street from the school for many years which it had sold some months earlier to help pay off the loan, but it only covered part of what was needed. On top of that, the same investors who bought that property were apparently now talking to the board, administrators of the order, and representatives of the bank that held the note about the possibility of buying the twenty-five acres that made up the Westthorpe Academy campus. Furthermore, they were apparently making an extremely generous offer that was becoming more and more difficult to pass up.

According to Joe's dad, the fact that people were interested in the Westthorpe property was not surprising. Over the years, the land there had gained value as attractive acreage for new housing due to its picturesque surroundings, proximity to the local train station, and easy access to the greater metropolitan area. What was curious to Mr. Pryce was how anxious these particular buyers seemed to be and the somewhat inflated offer they were reportedly making. In addition, Mr. Pryce was also hearing that some of the members of the board, including some within the order, were leaning toward a serious consideration of what the group was offering. Many felt that perhaps this would be best for everyone, given the current financial situation with the school. Members of the order were seeing this as not only a way of getting out from under the school's debt, but also as an opportunity to use the additional funds from the sale of the property for other purposes within the order that were also in great need.

After hearing all this from his father, Joe sank low in the sofa he was sitting in. It was not the news he wanted to hear. "Mind you," his father added, "these are all things I am hearing secondhand and may not all be completely accurate."

"But even if only parts of it were true," responded Joe, "it doesn't sound good." Fortunately, his mother was visiting his aunt along with the other kids and was not there to hear the latest. It was agreed that both Joe and his dad would try and spare her any word of this, if possible, until further corroboration could be made.

"Hey, what do you say we turn on the game and take our minds off this for a while?" suggested Mr. Pryce as he turned on the TV.

"Thanks, Dad," responded Joe rather dejectedly, "but I think I'm going to head up to bed. I've got to get to Mass early tomorrow and then head over to Westthorpe for the Open House I'm helping out with."

"I understand, son," responded Mr. Pryce. "Look," he continued, "don't let this get you down. We've got to have faith and believe there is purpose in all things. Let's wait to see what happens and continue to hope and pray for the best. What do you say we go to the early Mass together in the morning and then stop at Minella's Diner and get a nice breakfast?"

"Sounds good, Dad," Joe replied, sounding very tired. "I'll see you in the morning," he added as he turned toward the steps.

"Get some sleep, son," said his dad as Joe slowly made his way up the steps.

~~~~~~~~

Joe opened the wooden door in the third-floor hallway of Moreau Hall. He stepped onto the landing just beyond the inside of the door that led to an old iron spiral staircase. As he held onto the railing that ran along the outer wall of the staircase, he began to carefully climb up the narrow steps. There was a faint sliver of natural light, probably coming from an upper window, that allowed him just enough brightness to be able to see where he was going.

The staircase creaked as he placed his feet carefully on each step. As he kept his right hand on the central column of the stairwell, he crouched a bit to avoid hitting his head on the bottom part of the stairs ascending directly above him.

He had been up these stairs once before during the family picnic that began the school year earlier this past September. Mrs. Palmieri, Westthorpe's director of public relations, had asked Father Sarjinski if she could get to the top of the tower of Moreau Hall to be able to get a bird's eye view of the picnic in order to take a picture for the school newsletter. Father allowed a couple of the students, including Joe, to join them in order to see the top of the tower for themselves.

Joe remembered the stairwell being much more lit up that time as he fumbled around trying to find a light switch, without success. He reached the floor after the first section of the staircase and was able to look out through two connecting windows directly across from the staircase on the opposite wall. He could see parts of the red tile roof and dormer windows atop Moreau Hall, as well as the tops of many of the trees behind the mansion. He also noticed there wasn't much daylight left and that cloud cover was making it that much darker. He turned back toward the staircase and saw the names and other markings scribbled on the walls and on a closet door of the room, no doubt left by students from years gone by who had wandered up these stairs much like he was now doing. It gave him pause to think that he was part of a long legacy of guys that had come before him here at Westthorpe, giving him a shared connection with them in all that he was now experiencing at the school.

As Joe reflected on these things, it suddenly dawned on him that he couldn't recall what had brought him up to the tower in the first place. At that moment, a beam of light from above him caught his attention. The light was coming from outside the door leading to the landing on top of the tower. Not sure what to make of it, he decided to climb the last set of steps of the staircase. When he got to the top, light was coming in from a small window just above the door that led to the outside and the top of the tower. He turned the knob of the door and pushed it open. He was suddenly struck by a bright, dazzling light that almost blinded him.

As his eyes slowly adjusted, the intensity of the light seemed to diminish somewhat as he began to recognize the distinct features of the top of the tower. He stood facing the parapet on the edge of the rear of the tower and could just make out the trees below and the tops of some of the chimneys of the old mansion. He stepped out further on the floor of the tower and turned to his left and faced the other side where the light appeared to be coming from. He shielded his eyes and looked up at what seemed to be the figure of a man. "Do not be afraid, my son, for I am a friend!" said a voice. Almost instinctively, Joe dropped to one knee and covered his face. A strange feeling of trepidation mixed with an increasing calm and peacefulness enveloped him. He slowly raised his head and saw what he recognized to be a Roman soldier standing before him, magnificently dressed in body armor covering a red tunic, with a sword and scabbard on his belt and a cloak hanging from his shoulders. He was handsome, cleanly shaven with brownish hair, and appeared to be rather young, perhaps in his mid-twenties. The light continued to shine all around, and there was a presence about him that suggested this was no ordinary man.

"Who are you?" asked Joe rather hesitantly, his voice breaking.

"I am George of Lydda," he said in a strong but reassuring voice. "I have come to offer you my help." Joe did not know what to say as he began to try and understand what this meant. "There are events transpiring that, if allowed to run their course, may very well lead to the closing of your fine school. But, I tell you, such developments may yet be altered. It is not too late for enough good people such as yourself to stand firm and take action." For Joe, although having been previously made aware of the reports of such a possibility, hearing of it now, spoken so plainly by the soldier, was a bit unsettling.

"But how do you know all this?" asked Joe when he was finally able to speak again.

"Through the prayers of many who have sought my intercession and countless others, we are very aware of such things," answered the soldier. After a brief pause, he then said, "For now, however, that is all that I can share with you. I must take my leave, for I have an urgent task to attend to for the King. We will meet again soon, I promise you. It will be then that you will be ready to hear more of what I have to tell you. Until then, I offer you my blessing and encourage you to keep the faith. To the King, be honor and glory!"

"Joe!" a familiar voice was calling. "Joe! Time to get up, son! You need to get up for Mass so you can get to the Open House at school later this morning, remember?" Joe's dad was surprised to see how difficult it was to wake him up this morning. Joe was usually pretty good about getting himself up, regardless of what time it was or what he needed to do.

"What time is it?" asked Joe as he tried to open his eyes and get the feeling back in his right arm on which he had slept.

"Just enough time for you to shower, get dressed, and be on our way," said his dad.

As Joe was finally able to get his feet on the floor, it suddenly occurred to him that he had experienced quite a fascinating dream. He normally wasn't one to remember his dreams that well, but this one seemed different. This one was much clearer and more vivid, almost as if it had been a true-to-life experience. He suddenly began to recall the details of the dream and remembered how the soldier had said he would be visiting him again.

Throughout the day, Joe felt the urge to tell somebody about his dream but decided it would be best not to—at least for now. People would think he was crazy, he thought, especially given what the soldier had said about there being a danger of Westthorpe closing. This was certainly not something his mother needed to hear about. Instead, he decided to conduct some research on the nature of dreams and seek information about his nocturnal visitor. Regardless, he also felt that, in the end, it was entirely possible that what he had experienced was merely an extraordinary dream and nothing more.

Chapter 6

WORKING STAGE CREW for the annual musicals at Westthorpe Academy was always fun, Joe had been told, so he had decided to sign up. As it turned out, not only was he working stage, but he had also been invited to play one of the "barricade boys" in the famous battle scene from the popular musical *Les Miserables*, which was scheduled for performances in the school auditorium in just a couple of weeks. This meant that not only was he working on helping build the barricade prop, he would also be acting in the scene itself—double the fun!

With all the time spent preparing for the performance, including keeping up with schoolwork and getting ready for the start of baseball season, not to mention preparing for the upcoming freshman camping trip, Joe was keeping plenty busy. In many ways, this was not a bad thing. When he was finally able to get home after a long day at school, which often stretched into the evening, he rarely had trouble falling asleep at night. This was very much welcomed because it had been a number of weeks since his dream about climbing the tower in Moreau Hall. During the first couple of days after the dream, he had found it difficult to sleep at all. But as the days went by and things started getting very involved with his schedule, it wasn't long before he was falling asleep before his head hit the pillow. After a while, he wasn't even thinking about the dream, almost as if it had never happened.

"All right, guys," said Mr. Capern, "let me have your attention." English Literature and Composition class was always fun with Mr. Capern. He had a good sense of humor and really had a passion for teaching. A lot of the guys affectionately referred to him as "Cap," but never in his presence, of course. "As we have come to understand throughout the course of the year, the common literary genres consist of prose, poetry, drama, and . . . yes, who can tell me what the last one is? Yes, Mr. Lee, I see you have a hand up."

"That would be nonfiction," answered Aidan Lee from the back of the classroom.

"Correct," responded Mr. Capern. It just happened to be the last period of the day on a Friday, and the final seconds of class were ticking away.

"As we wind things down today, guys, I want to wish you safe travels on your trip to Gettysburg. I look forward to seeing all of you back safe and sound in a couple of days. And don't forget—I want a full report on your visit to the Edgar Allen Poe House and Museum on your Baltimore leg of the trip! Enjoy yourselves!"

"Thank you, Mr. Capern," was heard from among many of the students. With that, the bell was ringing to mark the end of the school day. Joe had some work with the stage crew to get to but needed to leave early enough to get home and finish packing for the trip, including getting the tent ready. They would be leaving early the next morning, and he needed to have everything all set to go.

~~~~~

Joe was glad to have Father Sarjinski along for the ride as one of the chaperones on the trip. He was also there to help focus attention on some of the more spiritual aspects, something that was emphasized on every one of the school trips. During the bus ride, Father demonstrated his knowledge of history by telling the students how they would be going to Mass on Sunday at Saint Francis Xavier Church in Gettysburg which was used as a hospital during and after the battle He explained how the church featured stained glass windows that depicted the Sisters of Charity of St. Joseph's attending to the wounded after the battle. They had come up from Emmitsburg, Maryland, the same order begun by St. Elizabeth Ann Seton, the first native-born citizen of the US to be canonized a saint, and were among the first to attend to the wounded and dying immediately after the battle. "You see, back then," Father explained, "doctors often preferred the assistance of nuns because they had had centuries of medical instruction and experience and were the only trained nurses in the country up to that time."

The bus began turning off the freeway toward the Gettysburg exit. "We're not far from the campground now!" exclaimed Father. "In fact, we're going to be setting up our tents within a short walk of one of the more famous locations on the battlefield. It's a place where, today, you'll find a statue of a military chaplain by the name of Father William Corby, who happened to be a distinguished member of our school's religious order of the Congregation of Holy Cross."

"No kidding, Father—that's pretty cool!" remarked Pete Figueroa, who Joe had thought was still asleep in his seat.

"He was a chaplain of the famed Irish Brigade," continued Father, "and during the second day of the battle, the Confederate army was looking to overrun the Union line. As the two opposing lines were about to converge on one another in a place called the

Wheat Field, Father Corby climbed to the top of a large rock and gave the men general absolution, while also inspiring them with words of patriotism and bravery." Father Al then paused for a moment. "Many of those men gave their lives that day," he offered, "but their sacrifice was not in vain. Thanks in no small part to their efforts, the tide of the battle turned and eventually led to a Union victory."

"Here we are!" cried a voice from the back of the bus as they slowly pulled into the campground parking lot.

"Incidentally," remarked Father, suddenly remembering one more important detail, "Father Corby's statue is the only monument on the entire battlefield dedicated exclusively to a chaplain."

"Did he survive the war, Father?" asked Joe as he began to stand up and gather some of his things from his seat.

"He not only survived the war," added Father, "but later served two terms as president of the University of Notre Dame, and he went on to write a book about his service with the Irish Brigade, a copy of which I have at home."

After getting off the bus, the gear was unloaded, and the work of setting up the tents began. The campground was a pretty decent place with a basketball court, volleyball net, and a good-sized field for throwing a football or Frisbee disc. "Come on, Pryce," implored Vince Hamden, "we've got a basketball game to play! Let's go!" He grabbed a ball out of his bag and headed for the court.

"On my way!" responded Joe.

~~~~~~

Joe had learned from camping with his family over the years how to best avoid getting wet in a tent in case it rained. Putting up the tent correctly is essential to keeping everything dry. As predicted, the rain did come, but it wasn't as bad as it could have been. Only a couple of the groups sharing tents felt the need to seek refuge in the pavilion of the campground in order to keep dry.

As the week progressed, the weather improved, and everyone seemed to have a good time. On the last full day of the trip, the bus brought the group to Emmitsburg, Maryland, as Father Al had mentioned before, to visit the Saint Elizabeth Ann Seton Basilica, Mount Saint Mary's University and Seminary, and the National Shrine and Grotto of Our Lady of Lourdes.

Their first stop was a visit to the Saint Elizabeth Ann Seton Basilica, a large beautiful church that had been built near where Mother Seton had lived with her community of religious sisters. The school they started there marked the beginning of the Catholic parochial school system in the United States. After a tour of the grounds and an opportunity to venerate and pray before the altar where she is entombed within the basilica, the group got back on the bus for a short drive over to the campus of Mount Saint Mary's University.

Upon arriving, a beautiful gold statue of the Blessed Mother atop a large bell tower could be seen on the mountain overlooking the valley. A guide met them to take them up the mountain to the National Shrine and Grotto of Our Lady of Lourdes. He introduced himself as Alex and said he was a student of the university. With much enthusiasm, he wasted no time in asking everyone to follow him up a very steep path that ascended along the slope of the mountain between the campus chapel and the seminary building.

After a few minutes, they reached the foot of the bell tower and statue. As someone who would obviously be more accustomed to such climbs, Alex appeared to be the only one not out of breath. As he stopped, he asked everyone to gather around him. "This site," he began to explain, "where the university, seminary, and grotto are built, is called the Catoctin Mountain. The name 'Catoctin' is thought to come from 'Kittoctons' which was the name of the

Native American Indian tribe that lived in this region." Most everyone in the group was happy to stop to rest on the sloping hill. It also gave them an opportunity to turn around and see just how far they had walked up while enjoying the beautiful view of the valley below. "The Catoctin Mountain is also famous for Camp David, located only about five miles to the southwest of where we are," continued Alex as he pointed in that direction.

"Camp David? You mean the mountain retreat where the President of the United States sometimes goes on weekend trips?" asked Clayton Starks, always prepared to discuss anything having to do with politics.

"The very same," responded Alex. "Practically every president going back to Franklin Roosevelt has used the facility there and invited family, world leaders, and many other dignitaries to visit over the years."

"Cool!" exclaimed Clayton. "I didn't realize we were so close to it. A president's daughter was married there, a G8 Summit meeting happened there, and, of course, the famous Camp David Accords in the late '70s that established a framework for peace in the Middle East was held there as well," added Clayton, rather proud of himself.

"Impressive—you really know your stuff," remarked Alex. "The facility was originally referred to as Hi-Catoctin and was nicknamed 'Shangri-La' by the first president to use it, Franklin Roosevelt. The name David comes from—"

"I know," interrupted Clayton.

"Shouldn't we let the guide do his job without interruptions?" protested Blaise Stirling, freshmen class president and so-called "wonder-boy" known for being the most well-rounded student in the freshmen class, a natural leader, and liked by most everyone.

"That's quite all right," offered Alex. "I'm glad to see such fine students from an obviously good school who are being well-informed about the history of our country."

"You're only encouraging him," reacted Pete Figueroa. "He'll take over the tour if you're not careful."

"Camp David," continued Clayton, clearing his throat to show his displeasure toward his detractors, "was named by President Dwight D. Eisenhower after his father and grandson, both named David."

"You are correct again—well done!" responded Alex. "I bring Camp David up," he continued, "because, as you probably know, being from a Catholic school, our current president is a convert to the Catholic faith, only the second president to be a Catholic, the other being John F. Kennedy." He paused for a moment. "Late last year, while visiting Camp David, the president, rather quietly, stopped here to pay a visit to the shrine and grotto, along with his Secret Service detail. It happened rather suddenly and with little advance notice. Everyone on our staff had to scramble a bit, but it worked out fine. I was fortunate to be working that day and actually had a chance to shake the president's hand."

"No kidding!" responded Joe. "I don't think I remember hearing anything about that at all."

"Not surprising," noted Alex. "But I think that's the way the president wants it to be. He prefers to keep his faith personal and private, but it is obviously very important to him.

"So, as you can see, this is a very special place. The National Shrine and Grotto of Our Lady of Lourdes here in Maryland commemorates the events that took place in Lourdes, France where the Blessed Virgin Mary visited a poor peasant girl of the town in 1858 in a number of apparitions. She appeared in an area just outside the village in a shallow cave-like rock formation, or grotto, a replica of which is just up the mountain from where we're standing and is one of the oldest of its kind in the United States.

There were many things she shared with the young girl, whose name, incidentally, was Saint Bernadette."

"That's the name of my parish back home!" remarked Euly Santos.

"Very good," responded Alex. He continued: "Since that time, Lourdes has become a place of prayer, consolation, peace, and yes, miracle healings. The Church, with the assistance of independent doctors and scientists, has investigated dozens of cases of alleged cures attributed to Lourdes and has declared a good many of them as being inexplicable and beyond medical and scientific explanation. Today, there is a special medical bureau at Lourdes created specifically to investigate such cases.

"The shrine and grotto here in Maryland was constructed only twenty-one years after the events in Lourdes, France. Since that time, many things have been added and a number of improvements made to accommodate the many visitors who come here every year. But long before the shrine and grotto were here, it was recognized as a place of prayer and meditation by a number of people in the area, including Saint Elizabeth Ann Seton herself who visited here quite often."

Alex then invited everyone to help themselves to the many places to visit throughout the shrine and grotto. The chaperones announced that they would have an hour to look around, visit the various locations, and stop by the gift shop if they wished. Joe found himself walking up to the grotto and the large statues of the crucifixion at the farthest end of the shrine. As he explored some of the sites, he began to notice how quiet and peaceful everything was around him. Alex had explained that the grotto was a very special place for prayer and contemplation for its visitors. Joe could understand why.

Joe stopped a number of times to admire the many beautiful statues and mosaics, the rosary-walk, and a stations of the cross. He lit a candle at the grotto and spent some time there in prayer.

After a while, he began to realize it was probably getting close to the time to be heading back to the bus. He looked around and noticed there was no one else where he was. He began to descend the path leading down the slope of the mountain, and as he was walking past a small stone chapel, he suddenly saw a man on the path just ahead of him. "*Bonjour*, my son. God's peace be with you," the man said with a very heavy French accent.

"Thank you," responded Joe, and then, "Oh, hello Father!" as he suddenly realized it was a priest. He was a short, older man, wearing a rather weathered cassock with red buttons and a crucifix that hung down over it from around his neck. A black biretta hat covered his head, and his shoes were rather old-fashioned and looked as if they had been walked in over many rugged miles.

"Have you been enjoying your visit to our sacred mountain?" he asked.

"Yes, I have, Father. It's a really beautiful and holy place," answered Joe.

"This is my favorite place in the world," the priest said. "I have been to many places throughout Europe and America, but there is no other place that compares. I have been blessed to be a steward and guardian of this hallowed ground and have helped many a pilgrim who has visited here in finding solace, refuge, and peace.

"Do you know," he continued, "just a couple of weeks ago, the president of our country came here and visited this very chapel where we are standing. It was getting late, and the chapel was locked, but I was able to let him in for an opportunity to pray. He is a man with much on his mind and facing many difficult issues. We must continue to pray for him. But he is a man of considerable faith who places his trust in a higher power."

"Yes," replied Joe, "Alex our guide told us about his visit here last year."

"*Oui*, that is true," answered Father, "but I am referring to another visit he made. In fact, he has visited here a number of times, but unfortunately, I do not think he will be able to continue doing that, which is *bien regrettable*." As much as Joe was enjoying conversing with this charming and saintly man, he was beginning to wonder if his stories weren't becoming just a bit exaggerated.

"My son, I can see that you are a fine young man, and I will pray for you. Everyone has concerns in their lives that require God's help. You can be assured that there are many who are praying for you and your intentions."

"Thank you, Father," responded Joe. "I very much appreciate that."

"Before you go, though," added Father, "there is something I wish to give you." He held rosary beads in one hand, and with the other, he reached out to Joe's hand and placed in it a small medal and chain. Joe looked down at the medal and saw a familiar figure on its face. He turned the medal over to reveal the words inscribed on it: "Saint George, pray for us."

"There is no greater assistance you can receive than from the communion of the holy saints," said Father assuredly. "Seek their intercession before the King whenever you pray. They are there to help you. God bless you, my son. *Au revoir*."

As Joe looked up from the medal he had been given, the priest was suddenly no longer there. Where had he gone? He was an old man, so he couldn't have gone far. Joe looked around but didn't see anyone. He walked around the chapel, but there was no trace of the man. He stepped up to the door of the chapel to check inside, but it was locked. He peered through the glass panel of the door but saw no one inside.

"Pryce!" cried a familiar voice from below the steps leading up to the chapel. It was Coach Zimmerman, the PE teacher at school and one of the chaperones on the trip. "Where in tarnation have you been? Do you realize you have held up our departure and forced us to have to reschedule our dinner reservation at Texas Roadhouse?"

"Sorry, Coach," responded Joe dejectedly. "I didn't notice the time."

"I suggest you hustle yourself down to the bus as fast as your skinny legs can get you there!" barked Coach Zimmerman.

"Yes, sir. On my way."

Getting on the bus, Joe received the usual ribbing for being late you would expect from the guys. Fortunately, the bus driver assured everyone he could still get them to dinner without much delay.

As Joe settled into his seat, Fr. Sarjinski was handing out brochures of the shrine and grotto that Alex, the tour guide, had left with him to give to everyone. Joe couldn't stop thinking about the old priest he had met at the grotto chapel and all the things they had talked about, as well as the mysterious way he seemed to have disappeared. He opened the palm of his right hand—yes, the Saint George medal was still there. At least he had that, he thought to himself. He looked it over curiously and then placed it over his head and around his neck. "Saint George," he said, silently to himself, "pray for us."

He opened the brochure and began reading about the history of the shrine and grotto. In the early 1800s, a priest by the name of Father John Dubois started the idea of creating the grotto high up on the mountain that had become known as St. Mary's Mountain. He was the founder of St. Mary's College Seminary, served as its first president, and would later become bishop of New York. He had been appointed pastor of nearby Frederick, Maryland and enjoyed visiting the Emmitsburg area. He especially loved the beauty of the mountains there. The story goes that one day, while traversing the woods and walking up the mountain, he followed a bright light that led him to a particularly beautiful spot where wildflowers grew and a divided stream ran around a great oak tree. Under the trunk of the tree was a deep, naturally formed hollow that he initially marked with a simple wooden cross. This was the spot that would eventually become the grotto. Since that time, the holy place, devoted to the Blessed Mother, has been a beacon of light, hope, and inspiration to many who visit there.

As he looked more closely at one of the pages, he noticed the picture of a couple of other people who had contributed to the founding and building of the grotto and shrine. As he looked more closely, he began to notice that one of the pictures was a painting of a priest who, the caption explained, was Father Simon William Gabriel Brute de Remur who had come to this area in 1812. He was assigned as a teacher and pastor of Mount Saint Mary's College and eventually came to be the spiritual director of Saint Elizabeth Ann Seton, who herself had come to the area to begin a school and eventually a new religious order. According to the brochure, Father Simon spent most of his priesthood at Mount Saint Mary's until 1834 when he was appointed bishop of Vincennes, Indiana and died there a short time later in 1839.

As Joe continued to stare at the picture of Father Simon Brute in the brochure, he became more and more convinced that the priest he had seen at the grotto chapel just a short time before was the exact same person as the man in the brochure. The man in the portrait was wearing the exact same clothing—a weathered cassock with red buttons, a crucifix on a chain that hung down from around his neck, and the black biretta hat! In addition, the facial features could not be more similar! But how could this be?

Chapter 7

JOE WOKE UP LATE that Saturday morning, having returned from the freshman trip the day before. It had been a fun trip, but it was always nice to be able to return to your own bed again and catch up on some much-needed sleep.

Baseball practice wasn't until later in the afternoon, followed by stage crew after that. He decided he had time to do some research. The first thing he wanted to do was find out anything he could about the priest he'd seen at the grotto. He wasn't necessarily eager to talk to anyone else about it until he had an opportunity to investigate a few things for himself.

He pulled up the website for the shrine and grotto to see if there was anyone he could contact and ask questions. Under the listing of personnel, he saw the contact information and pictures of a director, a chaplain, a visitor assistance coordinator, and the people who run the gift shop. All of them were women laypersons with the exception of the chaplain, a priest who was considerably younger than the priest he had met.

He tried all of the numbers, starting with the director, but was not having success getting through to anyone. He finally called the gift shop. After a few rings, he was about to end the call, not having an interest in leaving a message, when suddenly a woman's voice, sounding somewhat out of breath, answered "Saint Bernadette's Gift Shop, may I help you?"

"Yes, hello," responded Joe. "I wonder if I could ask you a rather strange question?" There was no immediate response from the other end. "Hello? Are you still there?" asked Joe.

"Yes, I'm sorry. I was just a bit distracted," said the woman. "We're somewhat shorthanded here today, and I'm helping some other customers. Anyway, what can I help you with?"

"Yes," continued Joe, "I was wondering if I could ask you a rather strange question? The other day I was at the shrine and ran into a very nice, older priest near the grotto chapel who said he was a steward and guardian of the place."

"Yes?" she said.

"Well, anyway," continued Joe, "I've called a number of people trying to find out who he is. He didn't leave me his name, and I just wanted to follow up with him if I could. Do you know of anyone who works at the grotto who might fit that description?"

Joe could hear people talking in the background and the woman's voice telling someone she would be with them in a moment.

"An older priest who claimed to be a steward and guardian of the shrine?" the woman asked as she finally responded to Joe's question.

"Yes, ma'am," answered Joe.

"Well," she said, "I've been here for a number of years. and I know for a fact we do not have anyone on staff who fits that description. However, there are a number of volunteers who come here that may be connected with the university or the seminary and are not directly affiliated with the shrine, and there are certainly a number of priests who come here all the time, either individually or leading other groups. But what I can tell you is we do not designate anyone that I know of as a steward or guardian of the shrine and its grounds. We do have a director of the shrine, but all of the people who look after the grounds are volunteer laypeople." After a brief pause, she added, "I do hope that answers your question. Is there anything else I can help you with?"

"No, ma'am," responded Joe. "I'll let you get back to your other customers. Thank you very much for your help."

"God bless you," said the woman as she said goodbye.

Joe then turned his attention back to his computer. He found a number of sites on the internet that offered information about Father Simon Brute. He was quite a fascinating man. Joe read that he had been born in France and as a young man witnessed firsthand the horrors of the Reign of Terror of the French Revolution that included the execution of Catholic priests. His mother risked her own life to secretly shelter a number of priests in their home. Simon himself brought food and even smuggled in the Eucharist to priests being held in prison. Such events had a profound influence on Simon, and he eventually became a priest himself.

But first, he had decided to study medicine, and upon completion of his studies at the College of Medicine in Paris (the finest school of medicine in the world at that time), he emerged as the most honored student of his class. Facing a most promising medical career, Simon shocked everyone, including his mother, by announcing his decision to pursue the priesthood. He explained that as noble as it was to cure the illnesses of the body, how much nobler must it be to cure the illnesses of the soul.

Simon decided to join the Sulpician Fathers and was ordained a priest of the order in 1808. Having already established a reputation for brilliance, Simon was invited by Emperor Napoleon

Bonaparte to his imperial chapel, having earlier invited him to be the master of ceremonies for the Archbishop of Paris, both very prestigious positions. Simon politely declined both and chose instead to be a humble teacher at the Sulpician seminary. He was not interested in lofty posts or seeking personal ambition. He sought rather to be a foreign missionary in bringing Christ to others, perhaps to India or China.

But the foreign territory he would eventually find himself in would not be Asia but America. In 1810, Father Simon was directed by his order to sail to the Americas. He was assigned to teach at the first seminary founded in the United States, Saint Mary's College in Baltimore, Maryland, where he would also later serve, for a short time, as its president. After only two years, he was then directed to teach at the other seminary the Sulpicians had founded in America, which was Mount Saint Mary's College in Emmitsburg, Maryland. It was there that Father Simon met Elizabeth Ann Seton and they became close friends. She had come to Emmitsburg at the invitation of the Sulpician order to start a new school which became the first free Catholic school in America. As Joe had remembered learning from the visit to the St. Elizabeth Ann Seton Basilica, she had also started a new religious order dedicated to helping the children of the poor. It was the first order of religious sisters to be founded in the United States, the Sisters of Charity of St. Joseph's.

Over the years, Father Simon became Mother Seton's spiritual advisor while she, in turn, helped him in improving his English.

Aside from his teaching duties at the Mount, Father Simon spent much of his time visiting the homebound of the community, hearing confessions, conducting baptisms, anointing the sick and dying, and bringing the Holy Eucharist to those who were not able to attend Mass. On many occasions, he would walk for miles to reach those who lived on the outskirts of the area. He was often heard saying, "How wonderful the day of a priest."

Joe stopped reading for a moment and thought of the shoes the priest had been wearing—old and well-worn. But that could be true of a lot of people's shoes, he thought to himself. Regardless, he couldn't help but continue to wonder how these two men could possibly be the same person. He resumed his reading.

Fr. Simon especially enjoyed walking through the woods and mountainside where the grotto is today, where he would pray the rosary and read from his breviary. He believed God's presence was revealed to us especially in the beauty of nature. He would spend much time in clearing, preserving, and caring for the area of the grotto and is responsible for having established many of the paths that cut through the shrine and grotto today. Due to his love of the mountain and his devotion to the people who lived there, he became known to all as "the Guardian Angel of the Mount."

"Steward and guardian of this sacred ground," Joe said to himself, reminded of the words the old priest used to describe himself.

In 1834, Father Simon was appointed to be the first bishop of the newly established Diocese of Vincennes, Indiana, which was very much a wilderness territory at the time. Father Simon did not want to leave his beloved mountain home in Maryland, but with humility and obedience, he accepted the call. Though his leadership of the Diocese of Vincennes was short-lived, Bishop Simon Brute left a lasting legacy there, much like he did wherever he went. His hard work led to the tremendous growth of the Church there, now referred to as the Archdiocese of Indianapolis.

Joe was further fascinated to read how this humble but brilliant priest and bishop was once referred to by President John Quincy Adams as "the most learned man of his time in America." He was also famous for the collection of books he once owned that many considered to be, at the time, the most prestigious personal library in America.

Bishop Brute died in Vincennes in 1839. His cause for canonization as a saint of the Church was begun in 2005, which elevated him to the title of "Servant of God."

"Joe! You had better get something to eat before practice!" called his mom from downstairs. Joe had completely lost track of time.

"I'll be right down!" he answered.

As he got dressed and put his baseball gear together for practice, he realized his research had brought about more questions than answers. But for now, he had baseball, the musical, and homework to think about. The smell of Mom's good home cooking from downstairs reminded him just how hungry he was.

As he headed downstairs, his dad was watching the news on TV in the family room with a mug of coffee in his hand. "Hey Joe, you've got to see this. I know you were just there this past week," Mr. Pryce said.

Joe sat down next to his dad on the sofa. As they watched, the news anchor reported on a story of how a retired Secret Service agent had recently written a book that talked about how the president, who enjoyed mountain biking, liked to stray from his Secret Service detail on his bike around the confines of Camp David whenever he was there. According to the agent, the president especially liked to bike up to the National Shrine and Grotto of Our Lady of Lourdes, just above the campus of Mount Saint Mary's University and a short distance from Camp David, after visiting hours and when no one else was there.

"Well, what do you make of that?" remarked Joe's dad. "And to think you guys were just there. In a way, I think it's nice to know our president has a place like that he can go. On the other hand, giving the slip to the Secret Service detail, even for a short amount of time . . . well . . ." His dad paused. "Anyway, you can bet now that the word is out, he won't be doing that again anytime soon."

Joe stared at the screen. Again, he thought back to what the old priest had said at the grotto about how he had seen the president there on a number of occasions, having once helped him gain access to the chapel. And how he suggested that he didn't think the president would be able to do that for much longer. The news report seemed to confirm exactly what the old priest had said.

"Did you see the president on your trip?" asked Tess who was on the floor of the room playing a game with her sister.

"Yeah, what's he like?" followed Anna.

"What kind of bike does he have?" asked Bobby, who was watching the girls play.

"No!" remarked Joe, somewhat annoyed by the questions. "I didn't see the president, and I don't know what kind of bike he has. But, as crazy as it seems," he said quietly under his breath, "I'm beginning to think he and I may have a mutual acquaintance."

"What was that, son?" asked his dad.

"Oh, nothing important," remarked Joe as he headed to the kitchen for some breakfast.

Chapter 8

MR. TAPPER MET THE MEN at the front door of Moreau Hall. To say he wasn't particularly thrilled to see them again would be an understatement. He had been instructed by Dr. Nichols to allow the men to gain entry into any part of the building they deemed necessary in order to conduct, as it was being referred to, a "look around." This was their third visit to the school within the last couple of weeks.

Mr. Tapper was the Facilities Director for the school and was responsible for the maintenance and upkeep of all school property and grounds as well as the proper functioning of all building systems. Father Sarjinski affectionately referred to Mr. Tapper as "Saint Pete" — the man with the keys who possesses the power to open every door and lock in the school. Just as Christ had given the keys to the Kingdom of Heaven on earth to St. Peter, the head of the apostles, so too did Mr. Tapper have a similar responsibility as it related to the goings-on at Westthorpe Academy. It was always a comforting sound to hear the jingling of those keys and know that Mr. Tapper was around.

He took great pride in his work and considered the Westthorpe campus his baby. He enjoyed what he did and was well-liked by everyone connected to the school. When you met Mr. Tapper, you immediately understood why. He always greeted you with a friendly hello and a smile on his face. He had a special connection with the students and got to know practically every one of them by name.

But this was different. The administration was not letting on about who these men were and why they were visiting. That didn't sit well with Mr. Tapper, who didn't like being underinformed, especially as it involved total strangers poking around the school. Sure, the mansion building itself was over a hundred years old and was in constant need of upkeep. But when a boiler needed maintenance, or a pipe required replacing, Mr. Tapper was always aware of it. However, he also realized there were things done and decisions made about the school that he was not always going to be made privy to and, as an employee, he had to respect that. It didn't mean, however, he had to like it.

And he also didn't like some of the things he was hearing through the rumor mill. The presence of these men only contributed to the kind of speculation that occurs when people are not given all the facts and tend to fear the worst. Some among the faculty and staff were suggesting that the administration was merely looking to upgrade and renovate some areas of the school and that they were inviting contractors in to explore such possibilities. There had been talk about a capital campaign to raise funds for such a project for the last couple of years. The most persistent talk, however, was not as optimistic and focused on the concerns people were having about the financial solvency of the school and whether it would even remain open. In recent years, for example, faculty and staff salaries had either not been increased at all or were only done at a very small percentage.

Mr. Tapper tended not to dwell on the negative, however. Life was too short for that, and as a cancer survivor, he knew a thing or two about fighting through adversity and always remaining hopeful, regardless of the circumstances. His illness had been a real test of his own faith and had initially caused him to question God after seeing the effect it was having on his wife and family. But after seeing how people prayed for him (especially to St. Peregrine, patron of cancer patients, to whom he had developed a special devotion) and helped raise money for his treatments and recovery, he knew that somehow God had a purpose in all things. He realized that with the love and support of his family and friends, he would fight this disease and appreciate every minute God would continue to give him on this earth.

He loved Westthorpe Academy. The Westthorpe community had always been good to him, especially when he was sick, and he would never forget that. Sure, he had been disturbed by Mr. Whitaker's sudden departure from the business office. He had always had a close working relationship with him and was sad to see him go, especially the way it happened. And regardless of whether Mr. Whitaker may have had a falling out with the administration, he also knew he had been talking about retiring for some time and was convinced that was the primary reason why he decided to go. Therefore, it was going to take a lot more convincing before Mr. Tapper was prepared to accept that the school would be closing anytime soon.

Although the men at the door had introduced themselves during their first visit, the only name Mr. Tapper could recall was Victor, the one who was in charge. Victor always wore a tie loosened at the top with his customary white shirt that never seemed to allow quite enough room in the front for his stomach. The other men (there were two others) wore casual clothing, with at least one of them looking like he might pass for a general contractor. They both carried flashlights, and one carried specialized equipment of some kind.

After they asked if they could take a look in the basement, Mr. Tapper led them to the interior door beneath the staircase of the main hall. It was an ornately crafted door with the Wallingford family crest and coat of arms meticulously carved into the wood. The men followed Mr. Tapper through the door and down the steps into the basement. They entered a corridor with pipes running along the ceiling that led to some other rooms. A number of these rooms were simply used for storage of all variety of things. One of these days, Mr. Tapper thought to himself, the school needed to sift through some of this stuff and have a yard sale. Surely, somebody could find something of value down here.

After looking around, Victor let Mr. Tapper know that they would be fine there for a while and wouldn't require his assistance. Reluctantly, Mr. Tapper agreed to let them carry on for themselves and told them he would check back with them in a few minutes. Victor immediately suggested that wouldn't be necessary and that they would come up and find him when they were done. Hesitating for a moment, Mr. Tapper finally turned toward the steps and made his way back up to the main floor.

After leaving the men, Mr. Tapper returned to his desk in the small confines of his office next to the maintenance area. He could hardly sit still in his chair as he thought about the men in the basement. There was something about them he didn't like. They reminded him of the kind of people he used to hang out with when he ran with the wrong crowd from the old neighborhood. Although that was many years ago, he could still remember the type. There was a look about them that gave him a sense that something wasn't quite right.

After following up with a couple of tasks he was working on, Mr. Tapper decided it was time to head back to the basement. It had been over an hour, and he was anxious to see what was going on. As he opened the basement door, Victor suddenly appeared in front of him, leading the rest of the men up the stairs.

"All we need for now," said Victor as Mr. Tapper stepped aside to allow the men access through the doorway. "Thanks again for your help," Victor continued.

"Is there another area of the school you were planning on seeing today?" asked Mr. Tapper. Part of him was anxious to see them leave, but another part was still curious and thought maybe he could observe them further.

"Uh, not today," replied Victor, "but we'll be sure to notify the school if that should change." And with that, they headed for the parking lot and were on their way.

It was strange, thought Mr. Tapper, as he watched the men climb into their truck. The three times the men had come, they had only visited the sections of the school that comprised the original buildings of the property that were once part of the estate—the carriage house which was now the chemistry lab and music room, the old horse stable, since converted into the school chapel, and, of course, the mansion, now called Moreau Hall. They had spent most of their time in the mansion, starting from the upper level and working down to the basement. Whatever was going on, he thought to himself, he couldn't allow himself to worry about things he had no control over. Besides, it was the business of the school and not his to be concerned with. He simply had to continue to do his job and trust that everything would work out, while leaving everything in the Good Lord's hands.

And for Mr. Tapper, that was all he needed to know.

Chapter 9

AS HE TRIED TO OPEN his eyes, Joe reached his hands up to shield himself from what appeared to be bright sunlight. He suddenly remembered a similar experience last summer at the shore when he had fallen asleep on his beach chair and woke up with the sun directly in his eyes. As he continued to adjust to the light, he began to look around and saw that he was again at the top of the Moreau Hall tower, this time seated in one of the corners of the parapet that surrounds the top of the lookout.

"May the Lord's peace be upon you, my son." It was a voice Joe remembered. "Please, join me." Joe got up slowly. He followed the voice from the other side of the center of the tower as the light dimmed just enough for him to see before him, once again, the Roman soldier. He was splendidly dressed in his military vesture and armor, as before. There was a radiance about him that was not the source of the light around them, but was only a part of it.

Again, rather instinctively, Joe bent down onto one knee before the soldier. "Arise," responded the soldier to the gesture, in a stern but gentle voice, "for you mustn't fall down at the feet of a fellow servant. We are obliged to worship God alone." As Joe stood up, he saw that the soldier was leaning with one foot above the other on the parapet, looking out above the grounds below. "My own life as a soldier involved spending many an evening atop a structure such as this. In fact, the tower of this edifice reminds me of the tower that protects Wallingford Castle in England, a country near and dear to my heart. I am honored by the fine people of that country in making me their patron.

"As a soldier with sentry duty, it was my responsibility to be on the lookout for danger and to sound the alarm should it appear. But as I ascended in the ranks, I was privileged to ultimately become a consul in the emperor's imperial guard. As a military officer, one learns not only how to respond and react to the threat of danger, but how to properly prepare to defend against it.

"The enemy can take various forms and move in diverse circles. We should not be ignorant of his devices. The written Word speaks of his subtle cunningness and deception and how he can be found even within the friendly environs of our own assemblies. Or he can show himself as the most menacing of creatures, as a roaring lion, as a serpent, or a dragon that threatens to devour everything in its path, something which I can speak of firsthand. But as it is also written, those who keep God's commandments and bear witness to the King and have faith in Him will endure.

"To do battle with the dragon is to carry the banner of the King, to put on his armor so as to stand firm against our adversary's tactics. For the battle is essentially not against flesh and blood but is a spiritual one taken up against principalities and incorporeal powers. We must be secured in the truth, hold fast to our faith as a shield, and carry the Spirit of God as our sword, which is His very Word and promise to us."

Joe was literally paralyzed, unable to move or speak, completely entranced by the soldier and the words he spoke. But as before, it was not fear or foreboding he felt, but rather a comforting peace and serenity unlike anything he could describe. Much of what the soldier was saying he recognized from Sacred Scripture and was not unfamiliar to him (thanks in no small part to his Catholic upbringing and education). But he also realized he had never heard it spoken to him quite this way before.

"My young squire," continued the soldier, "I have come to inform you further of the cause that you have gained at least some advanced knowledge of up to now. As I related to you in our first meeting, your beloved school is facing the prospect of closing its doors. There are events occurring that are moving rather swiftly toward such an outcome. But also know the course of these events is in no way inevitable or predetermined. The world is not ruled by a blind destiny or fate as long as man has free will. God invites us to respond to His invitation, to seek what is true and good so that we can know and love Him and one another. And through that love and service of God and one another, we live our lives in such a way so that one day we can experience the kind of joy and happiness that no one can take from us—together with Him for all eternity. And, as one who knows, and as Scripture so rightly tells us, it is that pearl of great price that the merchant finds and sells all that he has to purchase because it is worth more than anything else!"

Joe felt himself so transfixed by the soldier and his words that he was aware of nothing else. The mention of joy, happiness, and eternity was suddenly more than just words but an experience of which he was feeling somehow an increasingly penetrating awareness of. He was perfectly content to stay there. There was nowhere else he wanted to be.

Perhaps aware of this, the soldier continued. "I can only be with you a short time longer. I must also give you notice that there are those involved who are well-intended as well as those who are not, and that there will be certain perils to overcome. However, all you need do is believe in the One who gives you strength, and he will guide you on the right path. Do not be concerned unnecessarily with what you must do or say, but trust that you will be directed in what to do and say at the given moment."

The soldier paused and looked at Joe. "Also know," he said, with a sincerity and concern in his voice, "that you have my help and the help of so many others of my company. You have our abiding assurance of that!"

Joe looked at the soldier, whom he felt was becoming more like a friend than anything else. "Thank you," replied Joe. "I am curious, though . . ." he said in a sincere and deferential voice. "I can't help but wonder why me, and why this place?"

After another momentary pause, the soldier answered, "'O, the depth of the riches and wisdom and knowledge of God!' Scripture tells us, 'How inscrutable are his judgments and how unsearchable his ways! For who has known the mind of the Lord or who has been his counselor?' My son, God will often times conceal the mysteries of the Kingdom from the worldly wise and the learned and instead reveal it to the little ones. This is done because so often the wise do not see things as God does but rather put themselves and their interests ahead of others. The Gospels tell us of how Our Lord implored them to allow the children to come to Him, for the Kingdom of God belongs to them. He then said that whoever does not accept the Kingdom like a child will not enter it. For indeed, Scripture further reminds us, 'the foolishness of God is wiser than human wisdom and the weakness of God is stronger than human strength.'

"My friend, before I take my leave, I ask you to be attentive to the signs and voices along the way that will be harbingers of events to come. Take heed and respond to them as best you can." After a pause, he looked at Joe and placed a hand on his shoulder. "I myself am at liberty to divulge to you now one such sign to which you must listen very carefully. It is this—

"'They will come in their legions but have faith in yourselves and do not be afraid. Though the danger is real, you will need all the cunning to bring them to heel. But you shall overcome their power.'

"As I bid you farewell for the time being, I offer you my blessing and intercession before the Lord. I encourage you to pray often and to abide in the faith. To the King, be honor and glory!"

"Joe. Joe. How are you feeling?" asked a woman's voice. Joe tried to open his eyes. "Boy, you were really out and difficult to wake up," added the woman. "I'm sorry, let me turn that off," she said as she reached over to flip the switch on the overhead lamp that was shining in his face. Joe was trying to recall where he was and realized the woman was a medical assistant. The last thing he was able to remember was walking with his mother into the doctor's office to have his wisdom teeth removed.

"Well hello, Joe. How are you feeling?" asked the doctor.

"Na ba," answered Joe, suddenly realizing how numb his mouth was and that it was filled with gauze pads.

"Good to hear," responded the doctor. "Everything went well. We did have one tooth that was slightly impacted, but it wasn't really a problem. You're going to be fine. Just need to get home and take it easy for a while. Someone will be coming in to go over all the post-surgery information you'll need to take home with you. You let us know of any concerns or problems, okay?" He placed his hand on Joe's shoulder. "Take care of yourself," he said as he turned and left the room.

As Joe got in the car for the ride home, his mom was purposely not saying much, realizing Joe was in no condition to be carrying on much of a conversation. It gave him an opportunity to think about his dream. It was all coming back to him now as he began to remember some of the details.

He took out his phone and was suddenly remembering quite vividly the message the soldier had given him. Not unlike their first meeting, his recollection of this dream was also extremely sharp and clear. He was able to record the words from the soldier in the notes app on his phone with almost total recall. When he was finished, he looked back over the message which read:

"They will come in their legions but have faith in yourselves and do not be afraid. Though the danger is real, you will need all the cunning to bring them to heel. But you shall overcome their power."

What exactly the words meant, he could not be sure. But for the time being, he wasn't quite ready to be thinking about that too much as the effects of having had four teeth removed from his mouth were beginning to take their toll on him. In addition, he was going to have to miss tomorrow's baseball game, but there was nothing he could do about that. Hopefully by Monday, he thought, he should be better and able to play again. At least he had the weekend to recuperate. But for now, all he could manage to do was close his eyes and allow himself to fall asleep for the rest of the car ride home.

Chapter 10

PETE FIGUEROA WAS IN FRONT of Father Sarjinski's theology class, preparing to give his PowerPoint presentation. He had invited Joe to help by having him sit in front of the laptop computer and tapping the key to move each of the pages while Pete concentrated on the presentation and the notes on his index cards.

"Good morning, everyone!" said Pete in greeting.

"It's one o'clock in the afternoon, Fig!" announced Nate Silverstein from the student audience.

"Yeah, you're right—sorry," reacted Pete. Not the best start to his project. "Good afternoon," he said with a quick recovery. "My project today is on a brief history of our school and how the Congregation of Holy Cross has been an integral part of that history."

Despite the introduction, the remainder of Pete's presentation went along quite well. Joe found himself engrossed in the subject matter, especially when Pete started talking about the Wallingford family that once owned the Westthorpe Farm property that would later become Westthorpe Academy.

"The name Wallingford first appears in Berkshire, England, now known as Oxfordshire, where the town of Wallingford eventually came to be. Many years later, a man named Robert D'Oyley of Lisieux, fresh from having helped William the Conqueror in his Norman conquest of England, built a medieval castle whose name would bear the name of the town, Wallingford Castle." As Pete paused, Joe stared at the computer screen and suddenly recalled how the soldier in his dream had mentioned the same castle and how standing atop the tower of Moreau Hall reminded him of the tower of Wallingford Castle. Joe looked at the screen with a picture of the castle as it appeared today. Although the years had significantly reduced what was left of the structure, perhaps the best preserved and most conspicuous feature of what remained of the castle was the tower itself.

"Next page," said Pete. "Joe, next page!" repeated Pete more loudly.

"Oh, sorry," responded Joe, momentarily distracted from his duties as Pete's assistant as he thought about what the soldier had shared with him. Pete continued.

"When D'Oyley first arrived at Wallingford, he was not a particularly honest man, having acquired much land in the area at the expense of the Church. However, local Benedictine monks challenged him to mend his ways, and they prayed for his repentance. He suddenly became ill and was warned in a dream to repent and change his life. His health was restored, and he became a devout Christian and spent much of his time giving to the poor and helping build many churches and monasteries in the surrounding area. Next page." This time, Joe was paying full attention.

"Years later, after the death of Robert D'Oyley, his nephew, Robert D'Oyley the younger became an important ally of Empress

Matilda during her struggle to gain the rightful claim to the throne of England during the Anarchy Civil Wars of that time. He safeguarded her in his fortress at Oxford Castle, which is guarded by Saint George Tower." Again, Joe's ears began perking up.

"Upon hearing she was holed up in the castle, her enemies surrounded the fortress and threatened to starve out its inhabitants. Empress Matilda, with the help of a number of loyal knights, made a daring escape, rappelling down the wall of the castle. Dressed in white to blend in with the snow on the ground, they escaped at night and eventually made their way to the safety of Wallingford Castle. Those who saw them during their flight through the darkness thought they were seeing ghosts!" Joe could sense Pete was taking a certain delight in telling this part of the story.

"For the remainder of the war, Wallingford Castle survived many sieges but was never taken. Though Empress Matilda would never gain her rightful place as sovereign of England, her son Henry would when he was recognized as the rightful heir to the throne after the Treaty of Wallingford was signed, ending the civil war and allowing him to eventually become King Henry II of England.

"Through the years, Wallingford Castle became a favorite of many English kings and was considered one of the most powerful royal castles in all of England."

Pete's presentation continued up through the establishment of Westthorpe Academy and how the school property was eventually purchased and made into a school. The Wallingfords had purchased the property, known as Westthorpe Farm, from a previous owner and proceeded to completely renovate and improve the existing structure that would eventually become the mansion known today, parts of which were modeled after the original Wallingford Castle. James Wallingford, who built and owned the estate, had made his money in the printing and publishing business. He had a particular fondness for history and was especially intrigued with and proud of his family's heritage. Over the years, the Wallingfords also became art collectors, and the mansion became an accommodating place for their collection.

Although they were quite well-to-do, they, like many, took quite a financial hit during the depression of the 1930s. The story goes that Mrs. Wallingford's mother, the famous Madame Duchesne, who was a widow, died rather unexpectedly in the house and was very much grieved over by her daughter, an only child. After a while, Mrs. Wallingford could no longer bear to live in the house her mother had died in and moved out of the estate. It was not until the 1940s that the Wallingford family finally sold the property to real estate developers who parceled its many acres into plots of land for single-family homes.

Through the wishes of the estate, the mansion and its immediate surrounding acreage was not part of the sale, and its ownership was conveyed to a trust overseen by the people of the community. There was a great desire to preserve the house by the residents of the area, who had grown attached to the property, and due to its historic significance. Some of the money left over from the estate was set aside for the purpose of preserving and maintaining the property until such time as a decision could be made as to what would become of it. Some envisioned it as a community center or a retirement home, but for a couple of years, the house remained vacant until it was purchased by the Congregation of Holy Cross for the purpose of opening a school.

Pete's project concluded with a round of applause from the class. Father Al then asked for questions and comments about the presentation from the students, which prompted Tony Salvatore to raise his hand. Tony always had a way of livening things up, but it was usually done in a way that was tolerable and respectful enough.

"Yes, Tony," said Pete.

"Yeah, Pete, you mentioned Madame Duchesne who lived in the mansion and died there suddenly. Do you think that's the reason we hear the stories about her ghost lurking about the mansion? I've heard it said that when a person dies unexpectedly, their souls can often cling to this world, seeking to finish whatever business they hadn't had the opportunity to complete. What do you make of it, or is it just stories?"

After Tony's question, comments were suddenly heard from among the students in the room. "Yeah!" "He's right!" "What about it?"

"All right, calm down, gentlemen," announced Father Sarjinski, seated in the back of the room for the presentations. Father always encouraged discussions in class and allowed them to go just so far before sometimes having to rein them in, especially when it involved a question that required a sound theological answer from him. He wanted the projects to be opportunities for the students to choose from a variety of topics he would provide them with and, within certain guidelines and parameters, allowed them to take ownership of the project by researching the topic and submitting their work. Father Al liked to follow the presentations with a Q & A session, in part to make certain the students in the audience were paying attention and learning something from their peers.

"I would like to first thank Pete for his work on a fine presentation," remarked Father, which prompted another round of applause from the class. "In the time we have left, I also want to take this opportunity to respond to Tony's question with a bit of an explanation." After a pause, he continued. "In a way, it's a bit unfortunate that as good as Pete's presentation was, the questions ended up being more about ghosts than anything else," remarked Father.

"I didn't mind it at all, Father," responded Pete, followed by a sprinkling of laughter among some of the students.

"I didn't think you would," answered Father as he looked at Pete with a smile on his face.

"We've all heard the stories of strange sounds and goings-on associated with Moreau Hall over the years. Most, if not all of them, have a reasonable explanation, not the least of which has something to do with the fact that the mansion is a very old building. Buildings of any age develop strange noises and stories of occurrences that cannot always be fully explained. Add to that the long history of the house, with a mixture of intrigue, mischief, and the embellishment of storytellers, not excluding my own, and before you know it, you have the makings of a good old-fashioned ghost tale!"

"Yeah, but ghosts can be real, can't they Father?" asked Eddie Kezerian, who rarely said much in class unless something really piqued his interest.

"If you mean disembodied human spirits idly wandering about the earth, causing all kinds of bedevilment and fright, then we need to re-examine our catechisms. Have we not learned something from the study of our faith? Do we not know that at the very moment of our death, an immediate determination is made as to our eternal resting place?"

Again, Eddie chimed in. "Yeah, Father, but much has been written over the years about how people have experienced apparitions of saints and other people who have died."

"You are correct, Eddie," answered Father, pleased to see Eddie involved in the discussion. "But always know that such things only occur when God permits them to happen, and always with a specific purpose He has in mind. And always for the benefit of the salvation of human souls! Scripture reminds us that nothing can happen except that the Lord has ordained it."

"So what you're saying, Father, is that departed souls can appear to the living when God so wills it, right?" asked Pete Figueroa.

"Yes, but only done with a particular purpose that He has determined is for our eternal benefit," answered Father Al.

"Perhaps the stories involving Madame Duchesne may have some truth to them after all," suggested Pete. "Maybe God has a special purpose in mind in having her return to the mansion. Could there be something she is trying to tell us, something important?" he asked.

"Like what?" responded Tony.

"I don't know," answered Pete, "but I think I might have to ask Mr. Warwick a few more questions."

"As I have mentioned to you before, be careful with anything Mr. Warwick might tell you, including what you have already heard," alerted Father. "As much as we all like Mr. Warwick and enjoy his sense of humor, I think he gets more mileage out of the Madame Duchesne lore than anyone I know. He rather enjoys getting a rise out of his students and seeing their reactions whenever he mentions her name. He's an alum who was taught by some of the first priests and brothers of the order who taught here and lived in the upper residences of Moreau Hall, filling Mr. Warwick's head with all sorts of stories."

With that, the bell to end the period was ringing. "Gentlemen, we will continue with our scheduled presentations tomorrow," said Father as the boys began to gather their things. "Until then, go in peace."

Chapter 11

JOE HAD ASKED HIS DAD to drop him off early at school that morning. A couple of his teachers had promised he could meet with them before homeroom for a few minutes to go over some things in preparation for tests scheduled for later in the week. His dad was also anxious to get into the office early that morning. Knowing this, Joe persuaded his dad to drop him off a short distance from the entrance to school on the main road to save his father the trouble of driving him all the way down the long driveway to the front door. Mr. Pryce said it was not a problem, but Joe insisted. "Thanks, Dad. See you tonight!" Joe said as he shut the passenger side door and waved to his father.

Joe didn't mind the walk. In fact, he rather enjoyed such occasions. It was still early dawn, and the moon and even a couple of stars were still visible in the clear sky. A spectacular mixture of rose, purple, and orange color was beginning to be seen in the eastern sky just above the trees, heralding the approach of a new sunrise. Joe could hear the chirping of the first birds of the morning as he walked across the soccer field, his shoes collecting some of the moisture from the dew still remaining on the grass. On the other side of the driveway, among some of the lower hanging trees and smaller bushes, he could see a number of deer who were enjoying the stillness and tranquility of the school grounds. A little further up and to his left was a groundhog who, suddenly, aware of Joe's presence, remained frozen, almost as if he were a statue.

As he approached the school buildings, Joe could see the light from inside the school chapel—no doubt Father Sarjinski preparing for morning Mass. The light shone through the stained-glass windows, adding an additional display of colors to that which Mother Nature had already painted in the sky that morning. After realizing how briskly he had been walking, Joe slowed his pace until he actually came to a stop at the edge of the senior parking lot, propping a foot up on top of the curb. How often, he thought to himself, had he walked these grounds and played on these ballfields without taking the time to appreciate the beauty of the place. It was a moment for Joe to remind himself how much he loved the school and how fortunate he felt to be there.

Joe resumed his walk, crossed the side parking lot, and headed to the front of the main classroom building. As he looked up the slope along the front of the school, he noticed three men circling from the other side of Moreau Hall, a couple of them carrying what appeared to be some tools and other equipment. Usually, at this hour, only one of the maintenance employees was around to open the front door of the school and prepare the building for the school day. Not even Mr. Tapper, who devoted long hours at school, including many Saturdays and evening events, would be around at this hour unless there was a specific reason. The men got into a black truck and drove hurriedly past the front of the school, down the long driveway, and onto the main road. Rather strange, Joe thought to himself. Maybe they were contractors called in to do some work in Moreau Hall, like fixing that old boiler that Mr.

Tapper was always complaining about. Perhaps they had another job to get to, which would explain their hasty exit.

Part of Joe's reason for getting to school early that morning had to do with the fact that the entire freshman class would be going on a retreat that day. They would be visiting a retreat center not too far from school and were scheduled to return by the end of the school day. He would then have baseball practice, immediately followed by stage crew. He knew that if he didn't get some work done that morning, it was going to be difficult finding enough time to prepare for those upcoming tests and finish his homework.

As he turned toward the entrance to school, a car pulled up in front parking lot whose owner he immediately recognized. "Well, good morning, Mr. Pryce. How are we this fine day?" said Mr. Hutcheon as he shut the driver side door behind him. Carrying his leather satchel bag in one hand, he pushed the button of his key to lock his car with the other.

"Good morning, Mr. Hutcheon. Thanks for meeting me this morning to go over some things."

"Not a problem. I'm usually here pretty early most days anyway." Mr. Hutcheon taught science and math at Westthorpe, having retired from many years of teaching in the public school system. He was now well along at Westthorpe, close to ten years, but was showing no signs of slowing down.

After finishing with Mr. Hutcheon, Joe hustled down to see if he could be one of the first in line in the cafeteria in order to get one of Mrs. K's delicious pancakes for breakfast. Joe had been in too much of a hurry that morning to have gotten any breakfast at home. "Mrs. K" was used in place of her full name, Mrs. Kostopoulos, and the students appreciated that. Mrs. K ran the kitchen and fed the students, faculty, and staff, mostly for lunch, but also provided breakfast in the morning. She always had a smile on her face and an encouraging word to say to everyone who came through the cafeteria.

"Hello, Mrs. K!" greeted Joe.

"Good morning, Joe," responded Mrs. K as she looked up from the register with her usual smile.

"I figured I'd come down and pay you a quick visit, seeing as we won't be here for lunch today," said Joe as he handed Mrs. K the money for the pancakes.

"Well, that's mighty nice of you to do that," answered Mrs. K, "although something tells me it was the smell of those pancakes more than anything else that brought you down this morning. I do hope you guys have a good retreat today, and please say a prayer for me and my family, will you, Joe? My daughter-in-law is about to give birth to our first grandchild!"

"That's great news, Mrs. K. I sure will. I gotta go—see you later," said Joe as he turned and quickly made his way out of the cafeteria and down the hall to see if his Latin teacher, Mr. Ronaldi, had arrived for their morning review.

~~~~~~~

The bus pulled up in front of the entrance to the St. Joseph in the Hills Retreat Center. After getting off the bus, the students were led to a large conference room where Father Al went over some things, followed by an opening talk describing what a retreat is all about and what the students should hope to get out of it.

The morning went along very well with group discussions, another talk by Father on spirituality, and the importance of prayer, Eucharistic devotion, and an opportunity for confession. After lunch, Father invited everyone to go outside and enjoy the grounds that surrounded the retreat house. He explained that it was an area of many acres, mostly covered by trees, with winding trails running throughout. Many of the trails, he explained, were lined with statues and mosaics of saints, and some had a stations of the cross for people to pray as they walk along.

The day had turned out to be sunny and pleasant as the boys ventured out in various directions. Some headed toward the large open field with a long, sloping hill in front of the main house. Most of the boys were simply satisfied to be outside and able to walk or even run around a bit, enjoying the natural surroundings. Joe was reminded about what he'd often heard his dad talk about—the importance of people needing to get outside more often, setting aside their electronic devices for a while and experiencing the great outdoors, what he referred to as the simple pleasures of life.

Father Al had also talked about this before sending everyone outside. He talked about how we can all discover God in his creation and come to a greater appreciation of how He speaks to us through the beauty of the natural world. He mentioned how the Pope had talked about this in one of his encyclicals and how a number of saints, most especially St. Francis of Assisi, enjoyed a great love of nature. St. Francis, he said, would take long walks through the countryside, admiring the trees, the plants, and the animals and seeing them all as a part of God's kingdom.

Still having some time left before Mass, which would be the last event of the retreat, Joe decided he wanted to explore some of the trails that Father had talked about. He had actually seen a sign as they pulled in earlier that morning that mentioned a trail that led to a grotto. Although he had come outside with a number of the guys, they had all scattered throughout the grounds by the time Joe decided to take his walk.

He found the sign to the grotto and followed the direction it pointed into the woods. It was a nicely paved asphalt path that gradually descended down a long, sloping ridge. The branches and leaves of the trees became thicker the further he walked and began to filter out more and more of the daytime sun. There was a connecting trail to his left that curved further into the woods and had markers for each of the stations of the cross running along its path. If he had more time, he thought, he might like to explore one of these other trails and pray along the way of the cross.

As he continued to follow the path, he began to see ahead and below him an opening in the woods where the slope of the hill appeared to level out. He walked farther to where there was a series of benches spread around a small natural pool of water and a connecting stream. He could see more benches further ahead, and to the left, all of them angled toward an area where two white statues were visible, one of a veiled figure and one of a lamb looking away from where he was approaching. As he got closer, he began to see that everything was facing toward a rock formation cut into a hill, forming a small cave-like opening where a statue of Our Lady of Lourdes stood.

He turned to his left toward the grotto and walked along a wider extension of the path made of dirt and small pebbles with green ferns to the sides growing wild all around. He could see now that the veiled figure of the other statue was a likeness of St. Bernadette kneeling before the Madonna. The place reminded him very much of the grotto they had visited in Emmitsburg on the freshman trip not long ago. There was a wooden kneeler in front of the Madonna, and Joe decided to take a moment to pray. It was a beautiful little spot, meant to be a place for quiet meditation and repose. A single votive candle was burning below the statue, suggesting someone else had been there recently. For now, though, the only sound he could hear was the steady flow of water that ran along the small stream between the path and the grotto.

After a couple of minutes, Joe began to have a strange feeling that he was being watched. He stood up and turned to look behind him but saw no one there. He walked to the side of the grotto and down to the lower part of the ground where the St. Bernadette statue was. As he turned his attention back toward the trail, he looked up and saw what appeared to be an observation deck high above the ridge on the other side, overlooking and facing the grotto. He thought he could make out a figure on top of the deck looking down at him. It appeared to be someone wearing a dark cloak with a hood, and rather short in stature. Not unusual, Joe thought to himself, to find people walking the grounds here. This is, after all, a retreat facility, and lots of people must come through here all the time.

Realizing it must be getting near time for Mass, Joe decided he'd better start heading back to the retreat house. He looked up again at the observation deck. Whoever he thought he might have seen was no longer there. Looking straight up the ridge, he considered climbing up to the observation deck himself, which would not only cut short his walk and save him time but would probably also provide him a very nice view of the grotto. Though it looked rather steep, he saw what looked like a very thin path to the right side of the hill that zigzagged up the ridge and eventually reached the observation deck. He decided to give it a try.

Following the path up the side of the ridge, he was able to reach the top without too much difficulty and took a moment to position himself on the deck of the overlook. Looking down, the grotto area now appeared very small. It was a beautiful view, and he was glad to have made the climb to see it. Stopping for only a short time, he turned and walked down the steps of the observation deck and picked up another part of the asphalt path that would lead him directly back to the retreat house. After only a few steps, he noticed a small pavilion with a simple A-framed roof situated to his right. Deciding to walk by it, he took a glance inside and saw what he guessed to be the person he had seen earlier on the observation deck. It appeared to be a short, older man wearing a black and somewhat weathered cloak with a hood over his head that covered most of his face. He was seated on a wooden chair, somewhat to the side of the pavilion, holding rosary beads in his hands, partly facing a statue of the Blessed Mother, and partly facing the entrance to what was a little outdoor chapel.

"*Tres bien, tres bien!*" the man suddenly exclaimed, seeing Joe at the entrance. "You had me worried you would not make it up, *la petite montagne!*" he exclaimed as he chuckled a bit. "*S'il vous plait*, sit down and join me." He remained in his chair but pointed to another chair not far from his. Joe immediately recognized the voice with the heavy French accent as that of the old priest he had seen in Emmitsburg. "It is good to see you again, *mon ami!*" said the old priest affectionately.

"It's good to see you, Father," responded Joe as he made his way to the other chair and sat down. The old priest was smiling from what Joe could see of his face, still partly covered by the hood of his cloak. As much as his outer garments were different, Joe looked down and recognized the same worn, old-fashioned shoes he had been wearing before.

"*Mon ami,* I know you are soon due to return to your friends for the Holy Sacrifice of the Mass, so I will not keep you long. I continue to pray for you and the effort that lies ahead in helping preserve your school. Our friend in arms and defender of the faith, George de Lydda, has given you counsel, and I am here to offer mine."

As he listened, Joe was beginning to feel a sense of relief in knowing that the old priest seemed real to him now, more so than from their first rather brief encounter. His mention of the soldier, together with the medal of St. George he had given him before, which Joe wore devoutly around his neck, gave Joe a sense of assurance. If heavenly assistance was something he was being asked to be a part of, he could not help but feel especially blessed, particularly knowing it had something to do with saving his school. And if it should turn out that all of this was nothing more than a dream, then all he could do was eventually wake up and have a fascinating story to tell.

"My son,' continued the old priest, "our most venerable friend, *Monsieur* George, has informed you of the acceleration of events involving your school. There is no need to burden you with details other than the following sign that I wish to leave with you today. *Le voila*: 'follow the lady who desires to help you. *Ecoute-la!* Listen to her! Seek the gift from beneath the loosed stone which encircles low the divine child who takes hold of the beast and triumphs over it.'"

Here was the sign, Joe thought to himself, that the soldier had promised would follow soon. He had put in his phone the message the soldier had conveyed to him, and he did the same with this. As mysterious as they were, he preferred to follow the advice of the soldier who said he should not be too concerned with what the signs meant for now, but should wait for the proper moment for an understanding of their meaning.

"This is all I can tell you for now, *mon ami*," remarked the priest. "You must go, or you will be late. As for me, I must return to my beads for there is much to pray for. Your president is counting on my prayers as are many others. It goes without saying that you are also included in my intentions as well."

"Thank you, Father," responded Joe. "And I'm sure the president could use those prayers."

"*Bien sur*," answered the priest, "and although his visits to the shrine in Emmitsburg have been restricted momentarily, I am confident he will return again, *tres bientot*, and I look forward to welcoming him."

"I'm sure you will, Father," replied Joe. "Father?"

"Yes, my child," answered the priest.

"May I call you Father Simon?" The more at ease Joe was feeling in the presence of the old priest, the more he wanted to ask him this question. He only hoped it wouldn't offend him.

After a short pause, the old priest answered, "Of course, *mon ami*, for that is my name, Le Pere Simon Brute de Remur. In fact, it's the name I prefer rather than being called 'Your Excellency' and all the other titles given to me when I became a bishop. *Mais, je vous prie*, do not misunderstand. Becoming a bishop is a great blessing, *un privilege extraordinaire!* But, I must say, I could not have been happier than being a simple country pastor and priest."

"Goodbye, Father!" said Joe as he motioned toward the chapel entrance.

"Au revoir, my son! God bless you!"

Joe bounded down the path and headed for the retreat house as quickly as he could. Upon reaching it, he opened the front door and turned down the hall toward the chapel. When he got to the chapel entrance, he looked in and was relieved to see that many of the students were still just now walking in, genuflecting, and kneeling before the altar in preparation for Mass.

As Joe walked down one of the aisles, he saw Father Sarjinski motioning for him to come over to where the side sacristy was located. As Joe approached, Father reached out and whispered to him, saying, "Can I count on you and Tommy Gans to assist me on the altar for Mass?"

"Sure, Father," responded Joe.

"Are you sure you're okay to serve?" followed Father, looking at Joe with some reservation. "You look like you've just seen a ghost! You and Figueroa weren't out during the break looking to see if the retreat house might have its own ghost stories, were you?" asked Father as his lip curled up on the side of his mouth, trying to disguise a smile.

"No, nothing like that Father," replied Joe, "I'm perfectly fine."

"All right then, gentlemen," announced Father, "let's get ready for Mass."

Chapter 12

THE CAR PULLED INTO the gravel parking lot as the headlights illuminated a sign that read "Park Closes at Dusk." Only one other car could be seen in the lot. Its lights were not on, but a dark figure could be seen inside along with the dim glow of the burning ember of a cigarette. A puff of smoke escaped the partially opened window of the driver side door.

Suddenly, a flicker of light passed through the window and out onto the gravel parking lot. The door opened, and a man climbed out of the car. He stepped on the half-spent cigarette on the ground, quietly closed the door behind him, and walked toward the other car.

"You're late," said the man in a somewhat hushed voice as he peered into the window and looked at the man in the other car.

"Sorry, but I had a few things to finish up at the office. Besides, having to meet you out here took some doing. My GPS had a hard time finding this place," responded Trent Petersen. Trent was a young businessman, working his way up the corporate ladder of the real estate investment firm Equity Properties.

"Look, Blackwell, I don't know why we couldn't meet over a scotch at the Turks Head Tavern where I know some other people were going."

"Keep your voice down," responded Blackwell. "That's precisely why I didn't want to meet there." Trent had known Gavin Blackwell since their undergraduate days at Drexel University. They had gotten to know each other when both were competing to be the dragon mascot for the university, famously known as "Mario the Magnificent." Gavin actually won the competition but only lasted a short time after realizing he wasn't as enthusiastic about doing it as he thought he would be. That didn't prevent his buddies, however, from referring to him as Mario from time to time which he wasn't particularly fond of.

Gavin had started ahead of Trent at Equity and was largely responsible for having gotten Trent a job there. They both had begun at the firm as legal assistants doing various tasks that included paralegal work, initiating title searches, and contract preparation. Gavin, however, had recently received a promotion with the title of executive associate, which expanded his job tasks to include property management and investment analysis and consultation. It really didn't do much to increase his salary, but it did give him greater access to the goings-on of the firm and an expanded influence in investment strategy planning and decision making.

Gavin Blackwell was a man in a hurry. He had decided at a young age he wanted to earn a lot of money, retire early, and turn the world into his oyster. However, he soon discovered that the real world was not always willing to cooperate with his plan. But he never let minor setbacks slow him down. He was always looking for a way to advance his opportunities, often times just barely within the margins of acceptable business practices and ethics. But because he could always be counted on to do the heavy lifting due to his ambition and drive, he was often times given enough slack to cut corners and get away with things as long as it resulted in increased profits for the firm. However, contributing to the improvement of the bottom line for the company was not necessarily resulting in any significant expansion of his own personal bank account, and that frustrated him.

"Come on," whispered Blackwell, "there's a pavilion over there where we can sit and talk." Trent followed Blackwell to a picnic table where they sat down. "I'll get right to the point," said Blackwell. "It's about the Westthorpe Academy deal."

"What about it?" asked Trent.

"I've been encouraging the firm to purchase the property—twenty-five acres of prime land suitable for a couple dozen single-family homes and/or townhomes," responded Blackwell.

"Tell me something I don't already know," answered Trent.

"Just hear me out," reacted Blackwell. "The owners have been moving swiftly toward a possible agreement of terms for the purchase of the property. In anticipation of that, we have begun the process of a title search and have been conducting some preliminary inspections of the property."

"Sounds like they're pretty serious about selling," suggested Trent.

"A couple of weeks ago," continued Blackwell, "I came across some rather interesting information while working on the title search and making some other inquiries." Blackwell stopped for a moment and put a hand on Trent's arm. "Now, buddy boy, what I'm about to tell you stays tight with us. Nobody else can know about it, you got me?" he said as he looked Trent straight in the eye.

"Yeah, sure, not a word," answered Trent rather dismissively.

"Good," responded Blackwell. He went on. "It turns out that partial ownership of the property had been given over to a Madame Marie Duchesne going back to the early 1930s."

"Wait a minute," interjected Trent, "please don't tell me you invited me out here to this dark, secluded place for a history lesson about the 1930s when I could be at a happy hour right now having a good time." He looked down at his phone.

"I wouldn't drag you out here," responded Blackwell, "if I didn't have something I think you'd be especially interested in. Besides, I'm not one to waste people's time, especially my own."

"All right, I'll give you that," responded Trent.

"And yes, I'll buy you that drink just as soon as we're done here," promised Blackwell. "How's that?"

"Make it two," replied Trent.

"Madame Duchesne was the mother-in-law of James Wallingford, whose family had built the property," continued Blackwell. "Wallingford had lost a lot of money after the stock market crash that brought about the depression of the 1930s and early '40s. In order to save his estate, he invited his mother-in-law to take partial ownership of the property, which helped stave off his many creditors. She had apparently inherited quite a lot of money herself from her husband after he died.

"By all accounts, she was a rather shrewd woman who knew how to take care of her money, which is interesting because she had always given the outward appearance of someone who was merely interested in tending to her garden and living a secluded life. Unfortunately, she died rather suddenly herself. What was left of her own money conveyed to her daughter and son-in-law, but it remained tied up in the estate, which continued to struggle to pay off its debts."

"I'm curious," said Trent, interrupting, "It's one thing to conduct a title search, but it's another thing to find out some of these other things you seem to know a lot about."

"You're right," answered Blackwell. "The further I've looked into the various files and documents, I've had the occasion to speak with a number of area bankers and title companies, some of which still have a couple of old-timers in their employ. For a long time, the Westthorpe property meant a lot to the people of the community, and there are plenty of lasting memories. Some of these people waxed rather nostalgically about it and about Madame Duchesne, and that leads me to why I've called you here.

"A note was made on a document in some of the paperwork when the property was finally sold during the late 1940s. It's a rather obscure document that I doubt most people would even know existed. It was an attachment, somewhat like an addendum, a postscript, if you will, that had no bearing on the transaction and was technically not a part of the contract. It was handwritten, apparently by a bank officer, on the bank's letterhead. The bank itself no longer exists."

Blackwell paused.

"Well?" spoke up Trent. "Are you going to tell me what it said?"

"Incidentally," continued Blackwell, half ignoring Petersen's plea, "I should add that all outstanding liens, debts, and mortgages on the property were satisfied by the time the property was sold, thanks to the sale of a number of valuable works of art and, in no small part, to Madame Duchesne.

"The document revealed that sometime not long before her death, Madame Duchesne withdrew just over three quarters of a million dollars in cash from the bank as well as the contents of a safety deposit box registered in her name. No date of the transaction was provided. This was not an uncommon practice for people during the depression era at a time when banks were beginning to fail, and fortunes were lost. The document further states that this information had been previously noted some years earlier during the granting of probate in the administering of her remaining assets shortly after her death. I can imagine how serious concerns must have been raised at the time of the probate process because the document further states that there was no account of what had become of that money! A wealthy woman dies shortly after having withdrawn a considerable amount of cash from the bank, and there is no trace of it anywhere! This was duly noted again at the time of the sale of the property, probably out of a concern for any outstanding liens, mortgages, or debts that may have still existed on the estate and could later crop up. At any rate, what is important is the fact that there has been no account of what became of the cash, then or now!"

"Don't tell me you think that money is somewhere in the mansion?" blurted Trent.

"That's exactly what I think!" exclaimed Blackwell, becoming somewhat animated. "I am totally convinced of it! In fact, I don't think there's any doubt! Where else could it be? She died unexpectedly a short time after having withdrawn the money. She was, for the most part, a recluse who rarely left the house and spent most of her time tending to her garden. She couldn't have spent that kind of money in such a short period of time if she tried! Three quarters of a million dollars at that time would have been the equivalent of about twelve million dollars today. If that kind of money went somewhere, somebody would have known about it, even if she gave it away! Money like that doesn't just go unnoticed—unless, of course, it didn't go anywhere!

"And what about that safety deposit box? Think about what she may have been stashing in that. Perhaps some diamonds, jewels, an old coin collection, more money, who knows? But I'd sure like to find out! Something tells me the two go together—if you find one, you find the other!"

"Hold on," said Trent, chiming in, "even if it what you say is true, and that's a stretch, and even if you knew exactly where to find the money, how would you ever get your hands on it? You can't just waltz in there and start conducting a treasure hunt in the middle of a school!" He paused. "Wait a minute. I think I see what you're up to, Blackwell. I can tell when the gears are grinding in your head. You've already been scheming about doing something, haven't you?"

"All I've done so far," replied Blackwell, "is some investigative work, nothing more. But I do see this moving in a direction where I could really use your help and get you in on this. Think about it, Trent . . . if someone were to ever come across that money, it's probably worth a lot more than its face value. What I mean is, the currency of that era was probably printed and issued from various sources, including separate national banks. Many of those notes were only printed and issued for a short time, making some of them especially rare. Currency dealers and collectors pay top dollar for old money. The assessed value of old paper currency is determined by a number of factors that include the bank it was issued from, the denomination, the condition of the bill, and even the serial number on the bill. Any combination of these things can add considerable value to that money, which means this could be a motherlode of a find, maybe worth a couple million bucks or more!

"Don't you remember hearing the story, just a couple of years ago, about the contractor in Ohio who was remodeling a woman's bathroom in an old house and found about two hundred thousand bucks stashed in a wall. True story. It was all in cash, hidden in a couple of metal lockboxes hanging from a wire inside one of the bathroom walls. It had been put there by a previous owner, also during the depression era. When the money was uncovered, some of the bills were found to be quite rare and had an assessed value far greater than the face value, just like I mentioned."

"What became of the money the contractor found?" asked Trent curiously.

"A rather sad ending to that story," remarked Blackwell. "Unfortunately, the owner of the house and the contractor could not reach an agreement on how to split the money, so it ended up in court. After dealing with lawyers and court fees as well as living descendants of the previous owner of the house, all who claimed a share of the money, the woman eventually declared bankruptcy, and the contractor ended up collecting practically nothing while seeing his business ruined. Had they merely agreed on how to divide up the money, nobody else would have known about it."

"Which brings me to my next question," followed Trent. "Even if you were to find that kind of money in the house, don't you need to worry about some of the same things?"

"Relax, buddy boy. You worry too much!" remarked Blackwell. "First of all, there are no living descendants of the estate to have to worry about. I've done plenty of checking on that already. Madame Duchesne had only one child, and that was her daughter Mrs. Wallingford, who is also dead, as is her husband, Mr. Wallingford. In addition, they had no children. Secondly, I have every intention of gaining access to whatever is in there without it becoming public knowledge."

"And how do you plan to do that?" asked Trent.

"It's already being taken care of," responded Blackwell assuredly. "We've got access to the house through some of the preliminary inspections we've been conducting in anticipation of the sale of the property, which I'm in charge of. If the money's there, we'll find it."

Blackwell paused for a moment and then looked at Trent intently. "Let me ask you something, pal. Are you going to be satisfied working for someone else for the rest of your life, struggling up each rung of the corporate ladder, fighting every step of the way to achieve nothing more than a gold watch and a few stock options given to you at your retirement? And then, perhaps having only a few years remaining to even enjoy that?"

Blackwell stopped, got up, and started walking around the pavilion.

"Look, Gavin," replied Trent, turning toward Blackwell, "I've seen you operate before, and yes, perhaps you're right, maybe this could be something big. But I'm going to have to ask you not to tell me anything more. I'm not completely sure what you're up to and what you might already be doing, and I don't need to know. As far as I'm concerned, this conversation never took place. But I will tell you this—should you discover some further information that produces something more factual, more than just speculation and decades-old documents that don't seem to tell us much," he paused, "then, maybe, I might be interested, but only then."

"Fair enough," said Blackwell. "But don't miss the boat on this one, my friend. I've got a feeling this could be the jackpot we've all been looking for."

"We'll see," responded Trent, "but for now, I think you promised me a couple of drinks."

Chapter 13

JOE OPENED THE DOOR to the small private chapel of the priests of the Congregation of Holy Cross. It was in a corner of Moreau Hall just above the administrative offices of the school and just below the priests' residence. It was here that the members of the order celebrated Mass and gathered as a community to pray.

Father Sarjinski had agreed to meet Joe that late afternoon. Joe's scheduled baseball game had been canceled due to the rain, and he wasn't needed in the auditorium for stage crew until sometime later.

Joe knew the time had come to tell Father about what he had been experiencing these last several weeks. Part of him simply wanted to make sure he was sane and not merely hallucinating. But he also felt he was experiencing something that was important and yet was beyond his ability to completely understand. Perhaps most importantly, he needed someone like Father Al to help him discern that if what he was experiencing was of God, then what was God asking of him? He felt a sense of relief and anticipation in knowing that he would finally be sharing this with someone, especially someone he could trust and seek counsel in.

Father was seated with his head down, reading from his breviary, as Joe entered the chapel. He dipped his finger in the holy water font just inside the door and blessed himself with the sign of the cross as he genuflected toward the tabernacle. The windows of the chapel had most of their shades partially drawn, letting in very little light from outside due to the rain and overcast sky. Although it was a small chapel, a large red sanctuary candle burned prominently near the altar, reminding anyone who entered that the True Presence was there.

"Hello, Joe," said Father as he placed the bound bookmark on the page he was reading and closed the breviary.

"Hello, Father," returned Joe as he sat down next to him on the pew. "Thanks for taking the time to meet with me."

"Not a problem. Glad to be of help," responded Father. "I was especially sorry to see your game postponed today. I finally had some time this afternoon and was looking forward to getting outside and watching you guys play. Oh well, I guess I'll have to wait for the next one. So what brings you here this afternoon, my friend?"

Joe then proceeded to share the whole story with Father, beginning with his concerns about the school closing, to his dreams involving the Roman soldier, as well as his chance meetings with the saintly priest. He found his mind was surprisingly clear and perceptive in being able to recall everything that the soldier and the old priest had shared with him. Because he knew he could trust Father Al, he felt no anxiety or reservation about being completely open with him without fear of being perceived as crazy or delusional.

Father listened intently to Joe, without interruption. When Joe was finished, Father took a moment to reflect upon everything he had said. He knew Joe to be a fine, upstanding, bright, and faith-filled young man who had just shared with him a most remarkable experience. Throughout his years as a priest, he had had many people confide in him experiences of deceased relatives or answered prayers attributed to the intercession of certain saints. He had experienced some of these things himself over the years, to one degree or another. But what Joe was sharing with him seemed different. The things he was describing were extremely vivid and detailed.

He certainly knew Joe well enough and, although he was not a doctor himself, he had no reason to think Joe was anything other than the exceptional young man everyone knew him to be, perfectly rational and of a sound mind. As a priest, however, Father was trained to know that it was necessary to attempt to properly discern what Joe was experiencing in order to be able to offer him the best possible advice and counsel. He was reminded of how Scripture implores us to test all spiritual things to see if they are of God and retain from them what is good. As a general rule, he knew that if such experiences brought a person a feeling of peace and trust in God, then that was an encouraging sign.

"Joe," remarked Father, "what you've shared with me took a lot of courage, and I admire your fortitude. You described how you were concerned about how others might react to what you've experienced. That is perfectly understandable. To that point, let me say that what you've shared with me seems perfectly genuine and convincing. I cannot say exactly what it is you have experienced. But one thing I can do as a priest is offer spiritual direction that may help us both gain a clearer understanding of this.

"Thank you, Father," responded Joe, an unmistakable sound of relief in his voice. "I really appreciate that."

"Prayer, first and foremost, is vital," Father emphasized. "If this is of God, then all we need do is ask and trust in Him to show us the way. Continue your special devotion to St. George and Father Simon in seeking their intercession before God. These remarkable people, both in their earthly life and now, served and continue to serve the Holy One of God, their King, as you said they so beautifully referred to Him as, for he is indeed the King of kings and Lord of lords. In that service, I like to think that perhaps they are inviting you to cooperate with them in a way that is pleasing to God.

"And don't think I have overlooked the fact that Saint George is your patron saint, Mr. George Owen Pryce. I think there is plenty that can be said for that fact alone, wouldn't you agree?" Joe laughed and quickly thought how glad he was to have brought this to Father Al and how, perhaps, he should have told him sooner. Regardless, the advice he was offering him now was extremely comforting and beneficial.

"I must admit," continued Father, "I find his reference to Lydda fascinating. Not much of a completely factual history is known of St. George. As I recall, it has been suggested that he lived in Lydda, at least for a part of his life, and may have been martyred there."

"You're right, Father," responded Joe. "I did some research myself. Here, I have it on my phone." Joe read, "'Although little is known definitively about his life, some suggest St. George was born in the region of Cappadocia, Asia Minor, where his father is thought to have originated from, now a part of the country of Turkey.'"

"That's what I'm more familiar with in knowing about him," said Father.

Joe continued to read. "'Another argument claims he may have been born in the Roman province of Syria Palaestina, where there is strong agreement that he was raised at least partly in a city named Lydda where his mother was from. Lydda was the Latin name for the current city of Lod which is in present-day Israel.'"

"You've really done your homework on this—well done!" offered Father approvingly. "Just to add to that," suggested Father, "St. George is highly revered and venerated throughout the world and is the patron saint of a number of countries. If my memory serves correctly of my study of history, he was known to have been a distinguished officer in the guard of the Roman Emperor Diocletian. Diocletian, of course, became one of the most notorious emperors due to his ruthless persecution of Christians. His edict took away the rights of Christians and forced them to observe pagan religious practices. Many refused and were subsequently persecuted, tortured, and killed. The same edict extended to all Roman soldiers as well. George also refused to comply with the edict and publicly pronounced his faith in Christ.

"Because he was a valued officer, his superiors first attempted to change his mind by offering him money and property, but he still refused. They had no other choice but to arrest him, and he was severely tortured and ultimately executed."

"You really know your history, Father," responded Joe as he looked again at his phone. "Yeah, here's part of what you just mentioned," he said and continued reading. "'Many who witnessed George's martyrdom were so moved that it inspired them to convert to Christianity. One of them was Alexandra of Rome who, many claim, may have been the wife of Diocletian himself. This did not prevent her, however, from meeting the same fate as she was also martyred a short time later.' And anyone who knows Saint George," added Joe as he looked up from his phone, "must know the story of his slaying of the dragon." He read again. "'There are several versions of the story. One of them says that a princess was offered to a dragon to appease him after he threatened to destroy a village. Before she could be eaten, Saint George appeared and fought the dragon, finally running him through with a lance. George refused anything in return for saving the village other than to ask that people be baptized and accept the Christian faith, which they did. The dragon he slew is said to represent the enemies of Christ, which includes evil acts as well as the devil and his demons, all of which are ultimately vanquished by the saving waters of baptism.'"

"Indeed," responded Father. "That reminds me," he continued after a brief pause, "last year, I went on one of the school trips to New York. We visited the United Nations building, and in its gardens is a statue of Saint George that was given to the UN as a gift from the former Soviet Union." Father reached into his pocket and took out his phone. "I've got it here among several pictures I took on the trip. Here it is," he said and handed his phone to Joe.

The picture of the statue revealed the familiar image of St. George on his horse slaying a dragon. On top of his lance is a cross. The dragon itself is constructed in part with what appeared to be broken pieces of rockets or missiles.

"Yes, I remember now," said Father. "The statue was made by a renowned Russian artist, who, as I recall, is actually from the Republic of Georgia—not surprising!" Joe returned the phone to Father who again began searching for something on it. "Yes, here it is. The statue is called 'Good Defeats Evil' and was created by Zurab Tsereteli, a highly distinguished artist. I remember hearing of how he was inspired to do the work after experiencing a dream himself of seeing St. George slay a dragon that was constructed of scrapped pieces of nuclear missiles. This was not long after the US and Soviet Union had agreed to a treaty that would lead to the elimination of certain nuclear weapons. He knew then he had to create it.

"What I find remarkable about the whole thing," continued Father, "is how he took the idea to the leader of the Soviet Union, Mikhail Gorbachev, who approved it immediately. When the statue was completed, it was unveiled on the grounds of the United Nations. Imagine a work of Christian art from the Soviet Union, an atheistic Communist empire that had suppressed for decades the freedom of its people and that of many other eastern bloc nations, including, to a large extent, the free expression of religion. The following year, the Soviet Union collapsed, something I thought I would never see in my lifetime.

"Of course there were many other factors that contributed to that remarkable event, not the least of which included the papacy of Saint John Paul II, who helped inspire the Polish people to defy their government in breaking from the Soviet Union. One by one, other Eastern European countries followed, eventually leading to the complete dissolving of the Soviet Union a short time later."

"Not surprising, Father, that you would eventually bring up the name John Paul II, the great Polish pope!" remarked Joe with a smile.

"You noticed that," replied Father with a laugh. "I was hoping it wouldn't be so obvious.

"My point, my friend, is that I have no doubt of God's presence in the workings of human events, whether they be big or small. We see this in Sacred Scripture, and we see it throughout the history of the Church up to the present day. God is always present to us, helping us in ways that are often subtle but can at times be more conspicuous, never interfering in our free will but only asking us to cooperate in His, for He knows what is best for us. In this, says St. Paul, we should rejoice in knowing that God is near, never forsaking us.

"What all this means for you and for me, at this time and in this place, I cannot say for sure. I will say, Joe, that the warnings your visitors have apparently given you about our beloved school are very real indeed. Though I am not privy to any direct information, nor am I asked to offer advice on the matter, I do know that the administration has yet to offer any contracts to our lay teachers for next year. This is much later than at any time I can recall. Usually, by this time of the year, teachers are given an indication as to whether they are being invited to return again for the new school year in the fall. As a result, morale among the faculty and staff is really quite low."

"Yeah, we've noticed that about some of the teachers," remarked Joe.

"Rumor begets rumor," continued Father, "about how the school is looking to sell the property to an investment firm set on closing the place down and building single-family homes. I know we're in some financial straits right now, but I like to think there has got to be another solution."

"Prayer and trust, Father," responded Joe, "as you always say, and maybe a little help from some heavenly friends."

"You're right," answered Father, recovering quickly from a brief melancholy. "Let us continue to pray for that."

"Speaking of heavenly assistance," added Father, "there is something that I like to think might be of some practical help."

"What is that, Father?" Joe asked.

"Well, yes, you mentioned something the soldier had conveyed to you that he referred to as a sign, correct?"

"Yeah," answered Joe as he looked down on his phone again. "Here it is—'We pledge ourselves to hold this place. They will come in their legions, but have faith and do not be afraid. Though the danger is real, you will need all the cunning to bring them to heel. But you shall overcome their power.'"

Joe stopped and looked up at Father. "Is there something about it that makes some sense to you?" he asked.

"If I'm not mistaken," Father suggested as he looked at Joe rather pensively, "your soldier friend appears to have a particular fondness for musicals."

"What do you mean, Father?" asked Joe curiously.

"Those words," explained Father, "sound very much like a few select lines from the musical lyrics of *Les Miserables*, which is one of my favorite musicals, and, as you well know, happens to be playing in our auditorium next week."

Joe sat back in his seat, more than a bit surprised. "Are you sure, Father?" he asked.

"Yes, I'm almost certain. I've seen the production many times over the years, including on Broadway in New York. These words, even though they appear to be somewhat modified, and if I know the performance as well as I think I do, are from the barricade scene leading up to the battle in the streets of Paris."

Joe reached for his phone again and started pulling up the script from the performance, scrolling to the barricade scene. "Yeah, here it is," he said and began reading from it. "'Now we pledge ourselves to hold this barricade. Let them come in their legions, and they will be met. Have faith in yourselves and don't be afraid.'"

He suddenly stopped. "I think you might be right, Father!" Joe exclaimed. He read further. "'Let it be warned they have armies to spare, our danger is real. We will need all our cunning to bring them to heel.'" Joe stopped again, looking further down the script. "Yes, and here it says, "'We will overcome their power.'"

"There you go," remarked Father. "Although the soldier's words appear to be something of a variation of the lyrics, the comparison seems unmistakable."

"I think you're right," repeated Joe. Suddenly he was visualizing the scene in his mind where the revolutionaries and student ensemble pledge themselves to defend and hold the barricade against the enemy forces that threaten to defeat them. Joe had rehearsed the scene before, both as part of the ensemble and as a member of the stage crew, but had never really concentrated on the words, which are sung by someone else.

"Well, at least we have something to focus on," said Father.

Joe looked down at his phone again. "But, why would the soldier be giving us something from *Les Mis*?" asked Joe rather curiously.

"That, I cannot answer for you, my boy," responded Father. "In all honesty, I cannot pretend that the situation involving the future of Westthorpe Academy is not filled with great uncertainty.

I admit to being very much concerned that there are forces at work that are beyond my, or anyone else's, control.

"But, that having been said, I must also admit that what you have shared with me this afternoon reminds me that the Lord often works in ways that may be strange to us. Sometimes we forget that and think we must always be in control. I am reminded of the passage from the book of Psalms, 'Be still and know that I am God.' If what you have shared with me is truly of the Lord, then perhaps there are even greater forces at work that require us merely to trust. I believe it is the book of Proverbs that also implores us to 'Trust in the Lord with all your heart and lean not on your own understanding; in all your ways submit to him, and he will make your paths straight.'

"If anything, Joe, it is edifying to me to be a witness to your personal faith. You have obviously experienced something that has strengthened your belief and brought you closer to the Lord, and that is, indeed, a promising sign. As I shared with you earlier, I encourage you to continue to pray and have confidence that the Lord will make straight your path toward whatever He may have in mind for you. In fact, in most things, that is precisely what the Lord desires for all of us.

"Not to keep you much longer, Joe, but I would also like to personally add something else. Your resolve in the face of all this has had the effect of inspiring me to reevaluate my own previous complacency over what has been going on about our school. Up to this point, I have not been invited to have a say in whatever decision making is going on. Well, invitation or not, I am determined to change that. I don't think there is enough being said about why it is important to keep our school open and about why the Church, and particularly our order, is in the business of education in the first place. We need to ask ourselves why schools such as ours exist at all. Any school can teach the secular disciplines such as math, science, history, language, etc. But education of our youth needs to be more than just about gaining knowledge in order to get good grades, getting accepted into a fine college, or preparing for a promising career. Those things are certainly important. However, our mission is to educate the total person, in mind, body, and soul. It involves the instilling of values, the formation of faith, and the development of moral conscience, all within the framework of an inspiring and challenging academic curriculum and supported by a caring and nurturing faith community.

"It must also be about perceiving the bigger picture. A young person needs to see that they are a child of God, and that we are all made to be in communion with Him and each other, and that this is where our true happiness is realized. The young person needs to know why God has created each of one of us individually and for what purpose. The young person needs to know that our true vocation calls us to something beyond just this life. God calls each of our boys here at our school to one day be good fathers, husbands, brothers, and uncles as well as good lawyers, engineers, doctors, and the like. He may also be calling some to the priesthood and/or the religious life. It is through these vocations and professions that we contribute to the building up of God's kingdom in this life so that we may one day enjoy eternal happiness with God and each other forever in heaven.

"Our school strives to teach our students these things. And for the most part, I like to think we do it pretty well. And if we, and schools like ours, are not around to do these things, then who is?"

"That's the spirit, Father! That's exactly what needs to be said!" reacted Joe.

"I apologize, my friend. I think I may have gotten a little carried away."

"Not at all, Father," remarked Joe. "You've spoken the truth."

"Unfortunately, I'm not so sure what good it can do now," responded Father. "Nonetheless, there is a board of trustees meeting tonight, and I intend to be there. Beyond that, we will simply have to leave it in the Lord's hands."

"Do you think they'll give you a chance to speak, Father?" asked Joe.

"I suppose there's only one way to find out," responded Father. "Either way, my friend, it would appear that we are both on a course to try and do what we can to save our school. And, if you don't mind my saying, perhaps our situation is not unlike the young men at the barricade in *Les Miserables*. Like them, our cause is a just one, but we also realize the odds are not necessarily in our favor. Nonetheless, they need to see our resolve and know that we will not go down without a fight!

"Perhaps this is the meaning of the message, and that may very well be enough," concluded Father. "If anything, it has certainly succeeded in getting my attention!"

"Terrific, Father! This is inspiring! You've been with the school a long time and deserve to have a say in what's happening!"

"Well, Joe, considering your visitors seem to be inclined to be of help in this matter, then it seems perfectly reasonable to me to assume that Providence is on our side. And if that is the case, then who can stand against us?"

Father looked at his watch. "Our community is due in the chapel for Evening Prayer very shortly. Needless to say, I think we have much to pray for.

"Let's keep each other informed on this, Joe. I appreciate you coming to me and sharing all of this with me. I can only hope that I have been of some help to you. Above all else, keep the prayers going and trust that the Good Lord knows what he's doing. St. Paul says it best in his letter to the Romans—'We know that all things work for good for those who love God, who are called according to his purpose.'

"And please, do include me in your prayers about tonight's meeting. Something tells me I'll be walking into a lion's den."

"I sure will, Father," responded Joe. "But don't forget what you've taught us from the Old Testament about the story of Daniel when God sent an angel and saved him from the lions."

"You are absolutely right, my boy," responded Father with a chuckle. "I could certainly use the help of an angel tonight."

Joe got up from his seat and grabbed his bag. "I'll be praying for that, Father," he said. Good luck tonight. You're in my prayers. And thanks again for sitting down with me."

Father got up, and they both genuflected toward the tabernacle and then turned toward the chapel entrance. "And I thank you, Joe, for what this has meant for me. God be with you."

Chapter 14

JOE HAD GOTTEN A RIDE home from Stan Gilbeaux, a sophomore on the baseball team and also a member of the stage crew. "See ya tomorrow, Beau. Thanks for the ride," he said as he closed the passenger side door and turned toward the house.

Joe walked through the kitchen door and was greeted by his little brother Bobby, who jumped on his back, expecting to get a ride around the house like Joe was accustomed to giving him. "Hey Joe, take me for a ride!"

"Not tonight, little man," Joe said. "I'm beat, and besides, I've got a ton of homework I've got to get started on." Bobby slid down off Joe's back, a bit disappointed. "Don't worry, little man. I'll make it up to you next time, promise." Bobby was soon over the disappointment, running out of the kitchen and chasing after Anna, one of his sisters.

Joe walked into the living room. "Hi, Joe," said Kate, his kid sister. She was sitting on the sofa with a textbook and notepad on her lap going over some homework. "Dad's working a little late, and Mom got invited to your school's board of trustees meeting tonight. Apparently, the president of the parents' association couldn't make it, so they invited Mom to go in her place."

"Wow," responded Joe, "I'm kind of glad she's there. There might be some fireworks tonight!"

"What do you mean?" Kate asked.

"Oh, nothing really. How's everything around here?"

"Everybody's fine. I put a little dinner together for everyone, and there's a plate for you in the oven."

"Thanks, Kate. That's awfully nice of ya. If you don't mind, I might take it upstairs and finish some work I've got to get done before tomorrow. Don't worry, though. I'll come down later and clean things up in the kitchen."

"Don't forget this time, big brother. The last time you said that, you fell asleep in your room, and I got blamed for the mess in the kitchen." But Joe wasn't listening and had already walked back into the kitchen.

Joe opened the laptop on the desk in his room and placed a couple of textbooks next to it. Finally realizing how hungry he was, he ate the meal Kate had prepared for him rather heartily. After studying for about an hour, it wasn't long before Joe found himself beginning to fall asleep. He struggled to fight it off but quickly realized it was no use. He lay down on his bed and thought to himself that a couple minutes of shuteye was all he needed before he would resume his work.

Joe slowly opened his eyes, adjusting to the brightness of the light that shone around him. He stood upon a familiar perch, atop the tower high above Moreau Hall. He was looking out across the whole expanse of his school's grounds and the roofs of its buildings.

"It is a fine place, well worth preserving, don't you think?" said a familiar voice. He turned to see that the Roman soldier was standing to his side, not far from him.

"Yes, it is," answered Joe rather quietly as he stepped back and respectfully bowed his head.

"It was a wise thing for you to seek the counsel of your priest friend, my son. He is a good man. Prayers on his behalf are being answered this very night. For the Archangel and Defender of Heaven who vanquishes the dragon is with him. Although their work will be successful, it does not mean the task is complete. There are surrogates of the dragon that must also be contended with before the work is done."

"I only wish," responded Joe, "I could be there with Father Sarjinski. I feel helpless."

"You have done more than you can possibly know, simply through your prayers and the prayers of others," answered the soldier. "There are times when not only is that enough, but it is the best thing for us to do!

"You are young, and youth sometimes tends to want to hasten things along. I completely understand. But when I was not much older than you, I was given great responsibilities, and yes, I had my own moments of impatience. But I learned to trust in the One who allowed me to rise to those responsibilities and believe that He would guide me along the right path. I commend you, my son, in what you have been able to accomplish already. There will be no further counsel beyond tonight that I need offer you. In fact, the signs which have already been given you are sufficient for what lies before you. Trust in that and trust in the One who gives us everything we need.

"I salute you, my friend, as I would a fellow soldier, as one who defends against the adversaries of his King. And I will continue to intercede for you before the Throne as do so many others within the realm of the Kingdom. God be with you, my son! To his Majesty, be honor and glory!"

Tap, tap, tap. Tap, tap, tap.

"Joe, dear, are you awake?" asked Mrs. Pryce as she quietly opened Joe's bedroom door. Joe squinted as the light from the hallway entered the room as the door opened wider.

"Huh?" grumbled Joe. "What time is it?" he asked as he shielded his eyes.

"Not too late. It's about nine-thirty," said his father as he and Mrs. Pryce both came into the room. Joe sat up in his bed and slowly swung his legs around, placing his feet on the floor. He was still wearing his Westthorpe golf shirt and khaki pants.

"Sorry," said Joe, "I didn't realize what time it was. I was studying at my desk and started falling asleep, so I thought I'd lie down for a minute."

"Nothing to be sorry about, son," said Mr. Pryce. "We wanted to come in and share some news with you."

Mr. Pryce grabbed the chair in front of Joe's desk, moved it toward the bed, and offered it to Mrs. Pryce while he sat at the foot of the bed.

"How are you, dear?" asked his mom. "Things are so busy during the week that we hardly have time to sit and talk much."

"Yeah, sorry about that, Mom. You're right, things have been pretty crazy with school, baseball, the musical, and everything else. So are you guys just getting home?"

"Yeah, a couple of minutes ago," answered Mr. Pryce. "Your mom came in just ahead of me."

"That's right, Mom, you went to the board of trustees meeting," said Joe, suddenly remembering. "How did it go?"

"Well," she said, "that's what we wanted to come up and share with you. I think it's good news!"

"Really?" said Joe. "What happened?"

"Father Sarjinski is what happened," answered Mrs. Pryce.

Joe's mom went on to describe how Father Al had walked into the boardroom shortly after the meeting had begun and sat quietly until near the end. He then raised his hand and asked if he could say a few words. According to Mrs. Pryce, she cannot recall hearing a more impassioned speech in all her life. She mentioned how Father implored the members to consider anything other than closing the school and how he talked about the fine reputation the school had built in preparing its students to be good men and principled leaders within their future families and communities. He reminded the board of how important a school like Westthorpe Academy is in forming young people in the faith and why the Church, the community, and the world needs schools like Westthorpe.

"I could not have been more proud to be a parent of a son at Westthorpe Academy," said Mrs. Pryce. "I know you have always spoken highly of Father Sarjinski, Joe, and after tonight, I am absolutely of the same opinion! He was a real champion tonight! He spoke as if all of God's angels were at his side!"

Joe immediately smiled at his mom's mention of angels assisting Father Al. "And there's more," she said excitedly. "After Father Sarjinski sat down, a fascinating discussion broke out among some of the board members, including some remarks made by a couple of the representatives from the real estate investment firm looking to buy the school who were there. I must say, I found at least one of the gentlemen from the firm to be rather rude and unpleasant, especially after Father spoke. I believe his name was Mr. Blackwell. Anyway, all sorts of questions started being asked, some even directed toward Father. What a contrast he was compared to Mr. Blackwell. Father was polite, courteous, and a true gentleman whereas Mr. Blackwell was smug, abrupt, and rather surly.

"But here's the kicker, Joe," she continued, "something that made Mr. Blackwell all the more disagreeable. By the time the meeting was adjourned, there was a consensus among the board that there would be no further discussion of selling the school property for at least the time being, or until such time as other considerations could be examined effectively. At least that's a step in the right direction, don't you think?"

"It's definitely an answer to a prayer," said Joe, happily.

"Well, dear, we just wanted to let you know. We'll let you get back to your studies, but please, don't stay up too late."

"I'm fine, Mom," said Joe. "Besides, I had a nice little nap. Thanks for letting me know about the meeting, and I'm glad you were able to be there. We'll keep the prayers going that another solution will be found."

"That's exactly where your father and I are going now, to pray our rosary before bed."

"Good night, son," said Mr. Pryce. "Oh, by the way," he said, suddenly remembering something, "your sister Kate wanted me to tell you that she cleaned the kitchen and that you owe her big time!"

~~~~~

The sound of a vibrating phone could be heard on the truck console. Victor felt around for the phone, finally taking hold of it with his right hand while holding the steering wheel with the other. He took a quick glance at the phone to see who was calling. "Mario," he said and placed the phone to his ear. "Kind of late to be calling me, isn't it, Blackwell?"

"I thought I asked you not to call me that when we talk," said the voice on the line. "You never know who might be listening."

"Like who?" asked Victor. "There's no one else here in the truck with me."

"Just forget about it," answered Blackwell.

"I must admit, though," said Victor, "to being a bit curious about the name Mario. Of all the names available to use as an alias, you choose that one? Is it some kind of nickname? Where does it come from? Mario Andretti? Super Mario? What?"

"I said to forget about it!" repeated Blackwell, his voice now raised. "Besides, I've got more important things to discuss."

"All right," replied Victor, "don't get so testy. I'm listening."

"I need to meet with you right away, the usual place."

"Right now?" asked Victor.

"It's urgent!" replied Blackwell. "Ten thirty, be there!"

Victor was what you might call a jack-of-all-trades. He was pretty handy with just about any type of tool or machinery. During a stint in the in the army, he'd even learned a thing or two about explosives. At the moment, he was a private contractor who primarily did a lot of commercial building and home inspections as well as small repair and remodeling jobs. He had met Gavin Blackwell on a building inspection when Blackwell's firm was buying a commercial property. Since then, Blackwell had occasionally relied on Victor for advice and information on prospective real estate ventures as well as lining up the right people for rehab projects and other miscellaneous enterprises. Victor welcomed the business.

Blackwell had contacted Victor about the Westthorpe Academy property and, at first, merely asked him to begin a routine assessment of the mansion and the other buildings that make up the estate. Things suddenly changed, however, when

Blackwell began asking Victor questions about the latest technology related to scanning equipment and other devices used to look inside walls. Contractors rely on such equipment to detect wiring, piping, wooden studs, and such inside walls to make their work safer and easier. But of course, Blackwell let it be known to Victor he was looking for something entirely different. He realized he needed somebody like Victor, so he invited him in on the search for the money as well as a share of the take. Victor agreed to the arrangement but admitted to feeling less than comfortable with how much he felt he could really trust Blackwell.

The park had become a place where Blackwell could rely on having his clandestine meetings without fear of suspicion and free from any outside interference. As usual, Victor found Blackwell waiting for him in the pavilion. The only light was a dim glow offered by a distant street lamp along the road leading to the entrance to the park.

"Sit down, Victor," offered Blackwell. "You've got to listen to me very carefully because we've got to get moving on this right away!"

"Whad'ya got in mind?" asked Victor as he sat down across from Blackwell.

Some days ago, Victor had found an area in the basement of the mansion that appeared to be an entrance to a crawlspace which had been sealed off with brick many years ago. At first, he didn't think much of it, assuming there may be several reasons for why someone might want to do that. However, after having thoroughly inspected the other parts of the building using the latest commercial scanning devices and other imaging equipment and finding nothing, he decided to take a closer look at the brick wall in the basement. He drilled a hole through the brick and placed a micro inspection camera through the hole to look inside. Though it was difficult to know for sure, he saw what appeared to be a couple of metal boxes somewhat away from the inside of the wall. Unfortunately, a more definitive determination of what they were would be impossible without actually breaking down the wall. When Victor informed Blackwell of this, Blackwell wasted no time in assuming that this could very well be precisely what they'd been looking for. "There's only one way to find out," argued Blackwell, "and that's to go in there and get it! Now, we've gone over every other inch of the mansion, the carriage house, and the chapel and found nothing, right?" asked Blackwell.

"Nothing," answered Victor.

"All right, we've gotta do something with this as soon as possible. It's not looking like the sale of the property is as sure a thing as I previously thought. In fact, we may already be losing access to the building. I'm proposing we go in this weekend and get down into the basement. You've already told me that with a small explosive, we can put a hole in that brick wall, right?" asked Blackwell.

"Well, yeah," answered Victor. "Trying to cut through it is gonna take too much time. The only problem is, it's gonna cause enough noise that it can hardly be ignored."

"I've already thought of that," responded Blackwell. "We need to create a diversion so that a sound like that won't be as easy to hear."

"How do you propose to do that?" asked Victor rather doubtfully.

"I think we already have one provided for us. It's called *Les Miserables!*"

"Yeah, I've seen the signs for it at the entrance to the school," said Victor, "but how's that going to help us?"

"The performance involves an extended battle scene," explained Blackwell. "I went to the matinee this afternoon, and they really do some loud special effects that add to the scene, a lot of simulated cannon and musket fire and even some smoke. The sound of it reverberates all over the school. That'll be our cue to detonate the explosive.

"The plan is to do it this Saturday night, which will be the last performance. I'll be there again at tonight's show just to get the timing down. I've observed the school enough to know they probably won't be hiring out any outside security for activities like this other than having a couple of parents around to help. I'll call you sometime tomorrow night after the show and go over the final details. Have the materials you'll need and be ready to go. It'll be a simple operation, in and out."

"There better be some money on the other side of that wall, that's all I can say!" said Victor as he turned to leave the pavilion. "Don't you worry about that" replied Blackwell. "You just do your job."

Chapter 15

BY ALL ACCOUNTS, the *Les Mis* performances had, so far, been well received by everyone Joe had spoken to who had seen it. If they only knew the mistakes and miscues that were made, he thought to himself, they might think otherwise. But Joe was reminded by what his dad had said about how an audience doesn't really see or notice such things and views the performance in its entirety, which everyone seemed to be enjoying.

Tonight was the final performance which brought with it an excitement in knowing that the many days and hours dedicated to rehearsals, preparation, and stage construction were finally coming to an end. But it also brought with it an element of sadness that although the entire enterprise had formed many bonds among the people involved, it meant that everyone would eventually be returning to their own individual routines of life.

Saturday night's final performance also meant the long-awaited cast party after the show, which Joe was looking forward to. He liked the idea of finally being able to stop for a while and relax with his friends and everyone connected to the production.

He had to admit he was beginning to feel a bit overextended with everything going on. After all, tech-week had been draining enough with everything building up to the performances, along with schoolwork, baseball, and all the speculation having to do with the future of the school.

Joe also had something else weighing on his mind. After his talk with Father Al, he had been thinking about what Father had said concerning one of the signs Joe had received from the Roman soldier. Father had recognized it as sounding very much like the musical lyrics from the barricade scene in the performance. And because the show had two casts, Joe was on stage as part of the student revolutionary ensemble during the barricade scene in one performance, but then worked stage crew during the same scene in another. Throughout the first three shows, Joe had been paying close attention to the scene, both on and off stage. As someone who was in the performance, a part of him was hoping Father's speculation was wrong and that everything would go off without a hitch, like anyone would normally hope. But at the same time, if Father was right, he didn't want to miss whatever the sign might be and what it could mean.

Father Al had told Joe he would be attending each of the performances to see if he could be of help in searching for the sign. They agreed to confer after each of the shows, but neither had detected anything out of the ordinary thus far. Tonight, Joe would be in stage crew, which he was happy about because it gave him more of an opportunity to observe everything going on.

As the minutes counted down to the start of the performance, Joe looked out into the auditorium from behind the curtain. He was happy to see another large crowd beginning to fill the seats. He thought to himself that it really was a spectacular musical, set within a tremendous story of injustice that was redeemed by unconditional love. They had been discussing the story in Mr. Capern's English class, reading excerpts from the classic novel *Les Miserables* by Victor Hugo from which the musical was derived. As Mr. Capern shared with them, the story was, in a sense, a retelling of a Gospel truth of how hatred, bitterness, injustice, and revenge are transformed by grace, compassion, forgiveness, and generosity. The protagonist, Jean Valjean, who had already suffered a cruel fate, is taken in by a Catholic bishop who treats him with mercy and kindness. This, in turn, awakens in him a desire to extend a similar generosity in helping the woman Fantine, who soon dies but whose daughter, Cosette, Jean Valjean promises to look after and eventually raises. Later, given an opportunity to kill his nemesis, Javert, Jean Valjean instead shows him mercy and spares his life, like the bishop had done for him.

Near the end of the story, as Jean Valjean himself is dying, he is visited by two heavenly figures, the bishop and Fantine. They remind us of how the summary of our lives is found in how each of us responds to the grace God extends to us and how we, in turn, are called to be bearers of that grace to one another. As Hugo himself states in the novel and as is movingly sung in the performance, "Remember the truth that was once spoken: to love another person is to see the face of God." Perhaps Hugo's story is best summarized by his own words in the novel: "The book . . . is a progress from evil to good, from injustice to justice . . . from hell to heaven, from nothingness to God. . . The hydra at the beginning, the angel at the end."

"Come on, Joe," said Pete Figueroa, as he came up behind him, "we've got work to do! Curtain's about to open!"

~~~~~

The music stopped, and the lights slowly came back on to mark the beginning of intermission as a loud and exuberant applause was heard from the audience. Another good thing about final performances is that after all the rehearsals and three previous live shows, everyone had their lines down pat and is at the top of their form. The entire cast seemed to be feeling pretty good that night about the way things were going.

Despite this, Joe couldn't help but feel a bit uneasy. Coming up soon would be the barricade scene, and he kept running over in his mind the words given to him by the soldier. There had to be something more to all this, he thought to himself. Was there something he had overlooked? Had they already missed something from the previous performances? Suddenly Joe thought back to his last visit with Father Simon. He recalled how Father had told him to "follow the lady who desires to help you. Listen to her."

Joe had always thought of this as an encouragement to continue to direct his prayers to the Blessed Mother, especially under the title of Our Lady of Lourdes. He was more than happy to comply with such a request and knew there was no greater an advocate he could have than Our Blessed Lady.

But as powerful and effective as such prayer is, Joe couldn't help but think that maybe Father Simon's words had an additional meaning. Could "the lady" also be a reference to someone else? Another lady?

Sometimes the most obvious answers are the hardest to accept. As Joe continued to think it over, the only other lady that seemed to factor into this whole equation that made any sense, and the only name that kept coming to his mind was, of course, Madame Duchesne.

Could there be some truth about the Madame Duchesne stories? Was there something she was trying to tell us? Such questions merely added to the ones he was already trying to answer as they related to his own recent experiences. Perhaps the notion of having already been visited by two otherworldly beings should not be made all the more unbelievable, he thought, if he were to merely consider the possibility of another visitor. Besides, he was running out of time, and given whatever Father Simon was trying to suggest to him about a lady, this was certainly worth pursuing. And if this did have something to do with Madame Duchesne, there was no more likely a place she would be found than the mansion.

The lights of the auditorium flickered, indicating that intermission was coming to an end. Joe found Pete backstage. "Look, I can't explain right now, but just before the battle scene at the barricade, I need to head over to Moreau Hall. I'm not really needed here during the scene and, pretty much, for the remainder of the show. Just cover for me if there's any problem."

"Whad'ya mean?" asked Pete. "Whad'ya need to do?"

"I'll explain later," answered Joe as the music began to play and the show was starting up again.

~~~~~

The truck pulled up to the farthest stretch of the street where it came to a dead end. Victor had already turned off the headlights as the truck slowly pulled to the side of the road and rolled to a stop.

"Good," said Blackwell, "it's raining a little bit, which means nobody's gonna be outside to bother us." They were parked in the neighborhood of the single-family home community that surrounded the Westthorpe Academy school property. The houses were a fair distance apart from one another, and the area in front of them provided a sliver of land between two of the houses that led directly to the school grounds and Moreau Hall.

Blackwell had it all worked out. He had traversed and surveyed this stretch of land over the last couple of days to make certain their approach and getaway would go without detection. They would walk a short distance through some brush and a few trees, climb over a short, partly broken chain link fence, work their way through the old garden on the Westthorpe property, and then be in Moreau Hall. If everything went according to plan, they would get what they came for from the basement, make a quick exit, and be on their way in no time. After checking to make sure they had everything they needed, Blackwell and Victor got out of the truck, quietly closed the doors, and began walking toward the trees.

Despite getting a little wet and stumbling in the dark over some underbrush and a couple of fallen tree limbs, they reached Moreau Hall without too much trouble. Victor had become quite accustomed to the property by this time and had no trouble working the lock to the rear glass door. The building was dark, but there was just enough light from a streetlamp outside to allow them to find the door to the basement. They didn't want to use their flashlights until getting downstairs for fear of being discovered.

They could hear the sounds and vibrations of the musical from the auditorium, which was only one building and a hallway over from where they were. Blackwell was now very familiar with the performance, and even from this distance and noting the time, he knew precisely what part of the production was playing.

"We have plenty of time to get set up, but we better get started," he whispered. The door to the basement was not locked, and they closed it quietly behind them as they headed down the steps.

Flashlights now on, they reached the area of the basement where the entrance to the crawlspace was, covered by the brick wall. Victor went to work immediately.

"I'm heading back upstairs to keep an eye out," said Blackwell. "My phone's on vibrate. Contact me if there's a problem."

"There won't be a problem," responded Victor. "I'll let you know when it's ready."

Blackwell wasn't interested in knowing anything about the type of explosive Victor was using. He wasn't particularly knowledgeable about such things anyway. Victor was the expert in such matters, so he merely gave him the money to secure what was needed to do the job. Victor assured him he was only using what was necessary to create a large enough hole to be able to crawl through. Once through the wall, they would grab the boxes and get out of there. Though the detonation would be fairly loud, Victor was convinced the sound should not draw attention as long as the sounds from the battle scene of the performance were also being heard.

There were actually a couple of hallways and a short flight of steps that one could take from the back of the auditorium that connected directly to Moreau Hall. Blackwell was standing in the dark shadows of the hallway closest to the great hall of the mansion. From there, he could hear quite distinctly the sounds of the performance from the nearby auditorium. The time was getting closer to the barricade scene. He texted Victor but received no reply. Just as he was about to try again, he looked up and to his right and saw a dark figure approaching him. It was Victor.

"I've been trying to reach you," whispered Blackwell.

"The charge is ready," responded Victor.

"Good," said Blackwell.

The plan was to set off the explosive as soon as the battle scene began. Victor had to stand just above the basement door to detonate the charge. He had warned Blackwell there would be some smoke and dust for them to work through because there was little area for the smoke to escape. With that in mind, they had each brought a small gas mask equipped with goggles.

They were moments away from the start of the battle scene. Blackwell followed Victor back to the basement door. They reached into their backpacks, took out their gas masks, and put them on. Victor took hold of the detonator in both hands.

"When I give the thumbs up," instructed Blackwell, looking at Victor, "that's the signal to set it off." He took a few steps away from Victor, closer to the auditorium, and listened closely for the first sounds of simulated gunfire.

Chapter 16

JOE HEADED FOR THE DOORS in the back of the auditorium and through a door that led to the school hallway. Part of him was reluctant to be leaving the performance, but he felt he had no other choice. On top of that, he really wasn't exactly certain what it was he was looking for as he headed toward Moreau Hall.

He decided he would go to the congregation's chapel where he had met with Father Al some days ago. What better place to go, he thought, under these circumstances, but to pay a visit before the Blessed Sacrament in the tabernacle? He went up the steps and turned right, going up the side stairway that led to the third-floor residents. He stepped out onto the second floor, walked down the hallway, and entered the chapel.

The red sanctuary candle and a couple of distant street lamps from outside the windows were the only sources of light in the chapel. Joe actually found the setting tranquil and soothing as he knelt to pray. His mind turned to all the things that were going on, and he prayed earnestly that somehow a resolution to all of them would soon be realized.

Joe began to hear the faint sounds of the battle at the barricade from the auditorium nearby and could picture it in his mind. Suddenly, he was startled by what sounded like an explosion, followed immediately by a slight vibration. The sound, though somewhat muffled, was distinctly different from the sounds coming from the auditorium, unless the special effects boys had added something to the scene he was not aware of. He wanted to find out where the sound had come from. Sensing the source of it may have been somewhere closer to where he was and not from the auditorium, he decided he would go across to the main part of Moreau Hall and look there.

Joe left the chapel, reached the side staircase, and made his way down to the main floor. He turned to his right and began walking down the corridor toward the great hall of the mansion. As he turned the corner, the door leading to the basement suddenly flew open, and gray smoke began pouring out into the hall. A figure emerged from the smoke, turned, and looked at Joe, who was still a good many feet away. Another figure soon followed the first. They appeared to be two men, both wearing gas masks and carrying what looked like two large metal boxes. Joe stopped in his tracks in startled disbelief over what he was seeing. The two men suddenly turned and began swiftly making their way to the back of the hall toward the rear door.

Perhaps somewhat ill-advised, Joe's righteous indignation roused in him an immediate desire to chase after these perpetrators who had broken into his school. Fighting through the smoke, he went after the two figures, pursuing them out the back door and into the darkness outside. Once outside, he turned to his right and saw them running toward the side of Moreau Hall. Fortunately for Joe, the boxes they were carrying seemed to be slowing down their escape. Joe caught up to one of them as he ran down a set of outdoor steps that led into the garden. Joe reached out and caught hold of the man's backpack as they both stumbled forward into the center of the garden. Suddenly, Joe noticed another figure by his side as they both grabbed the man and tackled him. The man jerked forward and fell headlong into a low section of a circular stone wall, his head hitting the statue that stood in its center.

Joe fell into the plant bed surrounding the wall and statue. As he landed, the figure that had appeared at his side ended up right on top of him—it was Pete Figueroa! The man they had chased began groaning as he tried to pick himself up. He reached into a pocket and suddenly revealed a small pistol in his hand which he pointed at the two of them.

"You're gonna do what I tell you," he said, trying to catch his breath. "You're gonna walk away and not follow me." His words were becoming quite slurred as he began feeling the effects of having collided with the statue.

"Drop the gun!" demanded a loud voice from behind them. "Drop the gun and show us your hands!" Suddenly flashlights were shining all around. The man let go of the gun, drooped his head, and appeared to lose consciousness. Joe turned and was elated to see a number of police officers with their weapons drawn, circling all around.

"There's another one who ran into the woods!" exclaimed Joe as he pointed in that direction. An officer gave chase, followed by another.

"Are you boys alright?" asked one of the officers as he helped both Joe and Pete to their feet.

"I think so," replied Joe, brushing himself off a bit. "Boy, are we sure glad to see you guys!" exclaimed Pete.

Joe turned and looked up toward Moreau Hall and could see smoke escaping from the rear door as some people started milling about the grounds, wondering what was going on. Almost immediately, the police began cordoning off the area. Some of them were already in Moreau Hall securing the scene. The sounds of sirens could be heard, growing louder as they approached the school.

Joe turned to Pete. "What in the world were you doing out here?" he asked.

"Helping save your hide," answered Pete. "I got a little worried after what you told me backstage, so I figured I better come check on you."

"Well, I must admit," replied Joe, "it's nice to know I can count on the Figueroa footspeed when I need it!"

A tall man in a sports jacket and tie with a badge on his belt approached the boys. "Gentlemen, I'm Detective McFadden. First of all, I want to make sure both of you are okay. Do either one of you require medical attention?" Both Joe and Pete indicated they were fine. "I'm afraid we're going to have to ask both of you to stay right here for the moment until we can sort out a couple of things. Obviously, we're going to need to get statements from both of you if that's not a problem?"

"Not at all, Detective. We're happy to help," replied Joe. The detective took both their names and assured them they would let their families know they were okay. They asked that the boys not use their cell phones to contact anyone until such time as they had a chance to thoroughly brief them.

"I am curious, though," said Joe, "about how you guys got here so quickly?"

"I'd like to say we're normally that fast," suggested the detective, "but the truth is we got a tip from an alleged associate of one of these guys who apparently had a moment of conscience and let us know he thought something was going down tonight. His name is Trent Petersen. Do either one of you know him or have you heard the name?"

Both Joe and Pete shook their heads. "Never heard of him," answered Joe, "but we're sure glad he contacted you."

"You and me both," he replied.

By this time, paramedics had arrived and were working on the man they had tackled.

"Detective!" said a voice emerging from the woods near the back of the garden. "We caught up with the other one!"

Joe looked up and saw two officers escorting the other man, his arms being held behind him. With his gas mask now off, Joe immediately recognized him as one of the men he had seen leaving Moreau Hall some days ago when he had come early to school. He was brought over close to where the other man was. One of the officers put down a fairly large metal box on the ground next to another similar box that the man Joe and Pete had tackled was carrying. The boxes were old, dirty, and beat-up.

"He was carrying this," said the officer.

Both boxes had latches that kept the lids closed, but neither one had a lock on it. Detective McFadden placed a pair of latex gloves over his hands, pried the latches on both boxes, and opened the lids. "Well, well, I'll be!" he exclaimed as he looked through the boxes. "Let's see . . . breaking and entering, setting off an illegal explosive, reckless endangerment of countless people, stealing private property, threatening with a deadly weapon, and avoiding arrest, just to name a few serious charges, all for the sake of some lousy old tools!" The detective picked up both boxes, turned them upside down, and out fell exactly what he described.

"What?" declared Victor as he looked down at the boxes and their contents, not wanting to believe what he was seeing. He turned toward Blackwell, who was just regaining consciousness. "Why you lousy, dirty, rotten . . ." Victor started toward Blackwell but was quickly restrained by the two officers.

"Get them both out of here," ordered Detective McFadden.

Victor was led to a police cruiser while Blackwell was placed on a stretcher and wheeled into an ambulance under police guard.

Detective McFadden turned to Joe and Pete. "Thanks for your patience fellas. If you both could just sit tight for a little longer, I'll be with you momentarily."

"We understand, Detective. Take your time."

Both Joe and Pete were given a couple of blankets and some portable chairs to sit on while they waited in the garden. Fortunately, the rain had stopped a while ago, and they were made as comfortable as possible. Pete had plenty of questions he began peppering Joe with about what all this was about. Joe did his best to try to explain as much of what he knew as possible. However, he admitted to knowing nothing about who these men were that had broken into Moreau Hall.

Obviously, far too many questions still remained unanswered for Joe as well. Why were these men going to such lengths to forcibly break into the school? And what about everything that had happened up to this point involving the Roman soldier, Father Simon, and even Madame Duchesne? Perplexed, Joe got up and began walking around the garden, anxious about wanting to find answers to these questions. He said a little prayer to himself, asking his heavenly intercessors to help him sort through all of this. He decided he just needed to relax for a moment, patiently wait for Detective McFadden to return, and trust that somehow this was all going to make some sense.

"You know, it's funny," said Pete, as he got up and walked toward Joe. "That guy we chased ran right into the statue of *The Boy Strangling the Goose*."

"Is that what it's called?" asked Joe. It was about six feet tall and looked as if it had been a fountain at one time, which explains why it had a water basin connected to its pedestal. It appeared to be made of concrete and was showing signs of age and overexposure to the elements. It featured a young boy riding atop a large goose, with the boy's arms around the goose's neck. The goose, its beak pointing to the sky, struggled to escape, its wings fully extended, seeking to take flight.

"I must admit," said Joe, "the few times I've been back here and looked at that statue, I always wondered if the boy was just playing with the goose or wrestling with it."

"It just so happens," followed Pete, "that I did my art project in Mrs. Chiero's class on this same statue. She asked us to choose something in or around the school, reproduce it however we wished—as a painting, drawing, clay figure, whatever we wanted—and talk about it in a short paper."

"Uh-huh," responded Joe, knowing he was about to get an art lesson from Pete.

"I did a pencil drawing of it," said Pete. "It's hanging in the hallway right across from the art room."

"Is that really yours?" asked Joe. "I do remember seeing it— it's pretty good!"

"Thanks," responded Pete. "And there's a neat story about it. The Wallingford family, who owned the property, had quite an interest in art and collected several things over the years. Speaking of that statue, Mr. Warwick likes to talk about how it was probably a favorite of Madame Duchesne's—she spent a lot of time in the garden up to the time of her death. I've got the paper I did for the art project right here on my phone. I think you'd find it very interesting. Here, let me read some of it to you," he insisted.

"Yeah, I remember you mentioning before how they say Madame Duchesne spent a lot of time out here," said Joe. "But how do we know for sure she really did?"

"All you have to do," answered Pete, "is look around the garden and you'll find some of the trees with a little plaque beside them mentioning how she planted them."

"Really," responded Joe, quite impressed by Pete's answer.

"I've also heard Mr. Warwick say how she probably had a lot to do with the whole design of the garden, including the statue."

Joe was trying to put all the pieces together in his mind. For whatever reason, events had brought them to this place where Madame Duchesne spent a lot of her time. Obviously, this garden was very important to her. Was there something here that might offer a clue to solving this whole series of mysteries? And if so, what could it be?

A police officer arrived with two paper cups in his hand. "Hot chocolate for you fellas—compliments of a Mrs. K!" he said as he handed the cups to them.

"Fantastic!" exclaimed Pete.

"Please thank her for us," said Joe.

"Detective McFadden says he'll be with you guys in just a minute and apologizes for the delay," explained the officer.

"Not a problem," responded Joe. "We're fine."

"Now that you mention it, Pete," said Joe as the officer left them, "why don't you go ahead and read me some of your paper about the statue? Maybe there's something in it that might help answer some questions."

Pete took out his phone and began scrolling through it. "Here we go," he said. "'This particular statue is one of several versions of a most noted sculpture that dates back over two thousand years ago to a Greek artist named Beothus. Only a couple copies exist of the original, including one in the Vatican Museum. There is much speculation about what the sculpture truly represents. Some scholars suggest that the boy is not merely a playful child but is the personification of a child of divine origin from a mix of Greek and Egyptian mythology and that the goose is not just an innocent animal but a representation of evil that must be triumphed over.

"'Today, of course, such mythologies are no longer believed, but the Vatican Museum, and other museums like it, still value these fine works of art as a celebration of the artistic skills of those who created them. In addition, they tell us about the human struggle that has always influenced humankind in its search to find God. In the Acts of the Apostles of the New Testaments, St. Paul speaks to the Greeks in Athens and tells them that the unknown god that one of their pagan monuments represented is a sign of that same search which can only be satisfied in the one true God, a God not made of marble or bronze, but the one who creates all things and is close to us.

"'And that closeness reaches its fullest expression in the Incarnation. God does not denounce nature, beauty, art, or the material world, but rather redeems and transforms them into something greater by his grace.'"

"You wrote all this in your paper?" interrupted Joe. "I hope you got a good grade on it because it's not bad," he admitted. "It's almost as good as your religion project was," remarked Joe, somewhat sarcastically.

"Thanks, but let me finish," said Pete. "'Therefore, a work of art such as *The Boy Strangling the Goose*, though it may carry with it a mythological significance from the ancient world, can also speak to us today.'"

"Yes," interrupted Joe again. "We've been discussing things like that in Mr. Capern's class, such as when Victor Hugo in *Les Miserables* uses the term hydra, also from Greek mythology, to reference evil as represented by one of the beasts from the Book of Revelation in the Bible."

"I'm not quite done," said Pete, mildly irritated. He continued, "'The sculpture can carry with it a meaning that is perhaps even more significant for us today. The boy struggles with the goose as the divine child triumphs over the beast who emerges from the marshes that represent not only a refuge of evil but also our own daily struggles and selfish inclinations. It is a message of victory over evil and of rebirth into new life, which is fully actualized in Christianity.'"

"Wait a minute," said Joe as he suddenly stood up, reached into his pocket, took out his own phone, and started walking back toward the statue. He began reflecting on the words Pete had just read to him: *the divine child triumphs over the beast.* He looked down at his phone and read again the message Father Simon had given him.

"Seek the gift from beneath the loosed stone which encircles low the divine child who takes hold of the beast and triumphs over it."

Joe looked and noticed how a low stone wall encircled the statue from all sides. *Could this be it?* he asked himself. *Could this be what Father Simon was referring to?* He began looking more closely at the wall surrounding the statue.

"All right, fellas," said Detective McFadden as he carried a chair over with him and approached the boys. "I'd like to ask you boys a couple of questions. It shouldn't take long, and I'll have you out of here in a jiffy."

"Detective," responded Joe, "do you happen to have a knife or something like it I could use by any chance?"

"As a matter of fact. I do. Why?"

"May I borrow it for just a moment. I'm curious about something. And could you also bring over a couple of flashlights and a shovel if you can find one?"

Detective McFadden turned to one of the police officers and asked him to find someone connected with the school who could get them some shovels. He then handed Joe a rather large tactical folding knife from his pocket while he and Pete took hold of a couple of flashlights. Joe started poking with the knife around parts of the semi-circular wall, which was only a couple of feet high from the ground. After a couple of minutes, Joe discerned a part of the wall near the ground where there were some gaps between some of the layered stone and the hardened mortar. This small part of the stone wall appeared different as if it had been reworked. There was a large concentration of ivory-colored rounded stones all along the base of the statue. Joe began to remove a number of these stones from the spot where he was probing with the knife, exposing the ground beneath.

The police officer returned, accompanied by Mr. Tapper, both carrying a couple of shovels.

"Boy, am I glad to see you fellas are okay!" Mr. Tapper exclaimed, a look of genuine relief on his face.

"Thanks, Mr. Tapper. Yeah, we're okay, thanks be to God!"

"You're tellin' me," responded Mr. Tapper. "We were worried sick about you guys! And I have to tell you, I should of done something with those crooks the minute they first started poking around the school. I knew there was something I didn't like about them."

"It seems they fooled a lot of people," responded Detective McFadden, "the more we're finding out about them."

Mr. Tapper brought the shovels over to where Joe had been working the knife. They both began digging around the spot. After a while, they were hitting some rocks and began removing them as they went. Soon enough, they had managed to expose an area underneath the stone wall and began pushing their hands into the hole. They removed more rock but then saw what appeared to be an opening underneath the stone wall. Mr. Tapper reached into the hole and touched something that felt like some kind of garment with a rubberized feel to it. He couldn't pull it out, so he began digging more around the area, removing more rock. Finally, he was able to place both his hands on the garment, and he began feeling around it. It felt like it was wrapped around something large and fairly heavy. After a little more digging and removal of rock exposed a wider opening, both Mr. Tapper and Joe were able to start working the garment out of the hole along with whatever contents it was holding.

Pete and the police officer also began reaching down with Joe and Mr. Tapper in an effort to pull the garment out of the hole. After a little more digging and pulling, out of the hole came the garment and what appeared to be two fairly large grayish-colored lockboxes.

"What in blazes do you think this is?" asked Detective McFadden.

"I'm not exactly sure," answered Mr. Tapper as he wiped his brow with the back of his hand.

"I've got a hunch," suggested Joe, "that this might have something to do with what those two men were looking for."

"And whoever put these things here obviously went to a lot of trouble to preserve them," added the detective. "That looks to be an old raincoat wrapped around the boxes, no doubt to try and keep the contents as dry as possible."

Detective McFadden and the police officers tried to be as careful with the boxes as they could. To them, this was considered evidence that may have some connection with the events of that evening. Both boxes were old and weathered but were not damaged. The latches were tightly secured but did not appear to be locked. Again, with latex gloves covering his hands, Detective McFadden pulled open the latch to one of the boxes and opened the lid. He saw a large envelope resting on top and written on it was the name, "Madame Marie Duchesne."

Chapter 17

GAVIN BLACKWELL LAY in his hospital bed, intravenous tubes connected to one arm, while the other was secured to a raised bar connected to the side of the bed with handcuffs. In walked Detective McFadden.

"Well, Mr. Blackwell, how are we feeling?" Blackwell was still dealing with the effects of a concussion and was in no mood to talk. "Did you happen to see the paper this morning? I think you've far exceeded the fifteen minutes of fame that Andy Warhol said everybody would experience sometime in their life. Here, let me read a little bit of it to you." McFadden opened the paper and put on some glasses.

"Yes, here it is . . . let me read it. 'One of the perpetrators, a Mr. Gavin Blackwell, was arrested while trying to evade the police on the property of Westthorpe Academy. A student of the school by the name of George Pryce assisted the police in apprehending Mr. Blackwell. Up to this point, Mr. Blackwell's claim to fame had been that he was, at one time, Mario the Magnificent, the dragon mascot of Drexel University while he was a student there.'"

"Oh no," mumbled Blackwell.

"No, there's more," said the detective. "'You might say,'" as he read further, "'that this was a modern-day Saint George who has again defeated the menacing dragon.'"

"I've heard enough," protested Blackwell.

McFadden put the paper down. "I've got to hand it to you, though, Blackwell, and to the resourcefulness of that kid."

"Whad'ya mean?" asked Blackwell.

"Well, we know from the statements given to us by an associate of yours, Trent Petersen, that you were after what was thought to be quite a stash of loot in the Westthorpe mansion."

"I don't know what you're talking about," protested Blackwell.

"Unfortunately," explained the detective, "what you uncovered was nothing more than a couple of old toolboxes that appear to have been inadvertently left behind when that wall in the basement was sealed up many years ago. But the good news," continued McFadden, "is that your work was not all in vain. The irony, of course, Blackwell, is that completely unbeknownst to you, you led that kid directly to the discovery of something else."

"Detective," said a police officer who had just walked into the room, "they need to take him down to x-ray." Two attendants followed the officer and began wheeling Blackwell's bed out of the room.

"The discovery of what?" insisted Blackwell.

Detective McFadden turned to the officer. "Make sure he's secured at all times, and he's not to be spoken to until he gets back here."

"Understood," said the officer.

"Discovery of what?" Blackwell pleaded. "You've got to tell me!" he cried as he turned back toward the detective and was escorted down the hospital corridor.

~~~~~

"How did you know it was there?" asked his sister Kate. The whole family was relaxing in the family room, talking about all that had happened the previous night.

"Let's just say it was a bit of a hunch and an answer to a prayer, with a little divine intervention," responded Joe, revealing only as much as he felt was necessary.

"And don't forget my contribution with the statue of the Boy and the Goose," piped up Pete Figueroa. Pete had spent the night at the Pryce house and was now sitting in the breakfast nook, helping himself to the chocolate chip pancakes Joe's mom had made that morning.

"And not to mention remembering how you would tell me stories about Madame Duchesne and how she spent much of her time gardening," Joe reminded him, happy to give credit where it was due. "I figured those guys were obviously looking for something but that maybe they were just looking in the wrong place."

There was a knock at the front door, and Mr. Pryce welcomed the headmaster Dr. Nichols, Father Al, and Mr. Whitaker, the former business manager, inside. Joe was glad to see Mr. Whitaker again. Although everyone was a bit tired from the night before, they were all in good spirits and excited about everything that had happened. The phone had been ringing all morning from friends and family as well as reporters wanting to know more about the story.

"Joe," said Dr. Nichols, "we've come to thank you and Pete again for everything you boys did last night. In addition, we also wanted to thank you for discovering what appears to be a considerable amount of money that apparently belonged to

Madame Duchesne, the former matriarch of the Wallingford family that built and owned the Westthorpe Farm property. Thanks to you, it's looking like our beloved school will be able to secure its debt and remain open for years to come, God willing. In addition, the Congregation of Holy Cross order will also benefit from this sizable gift which will help provide for a number of its functions, especially in its missionary work among the poor, as well as in the formation of new vocations to the priesthood and religious life."

All of this was good news for everyone! After a while, Joe and Father Al finally had an opportunity to sit down in Dad's study and talk for a moment.

"I'm very proud of you, my boy," said Father. "Divine Providence has certainly played a hand in all this, thanks to your efforts."

"I don't know to what extent I can take any credit, Father," remarked Joe. "I do know you have taught us well. As the Gospel reminds us, 'we are but lowly servants; we have done what we were obliged to do.'"

"Amen to that," remarked Father.

"But I will say," added Joe, "it certainly does appear that Madame Duchesne had something to say to us after all, didn't she?"

"I can't argue with that, either," responded Father. "May God bless her, and may she now rest in peace. *Requiescat in pace*."

~~~~~

Gavin Blackwell would eventually heal from his injuries and would also learn to regret what he did. When he was finally told of the money found in the garden, he could at least feel some vindication in knowing he had been right about it all along. Unfortunately, though, that was about the only consolation he would gain from it.

The roughly three quarters of a million dollars that Madame Duchesne had withdrawn from the bank all those many years ago was still there, just as Blackwell had suspected. After all the money was counted, it turned out to be exactly $724,100. But that was merely the currency value at the time such bills were put in circulation. Many of the bills discovered were very rare, and some were worth considerably more, all these many years later. But that wasn't all. Also found within one of the boxes was an old collection that included a number of very rare coins of considerable value. Speculation was that this had been something that Madame Duchesne's husband had owned. This may have been what Blackwell was guessing was in Madame Duchesne's safe deposit box that she had also withdrawn from the bank those many years ago.

Although it was difficult to truly place a precise value on the entire find, one assessment placed its worth at as much as four million dollars!

Blackwell had also been right about something else. After a thorough search, no living relatives could be found that had any connection to the Wallingford family estate. It looked quite certain that all property of the estate, including anything found on the former Westthorpe Farm property, would rightfully and legally convey to the school.

Though Gavin Blackwell proved to be right on a number of things, he was wrong about what mattered most. No one doubts the importance of money. It is a good thing as long as it is valued properly. But if it is not, it can do strange things to people. The unbridled pursuit of it has plagued many a person throughout human history. Money as a means to an end is a good thing, but the love of money, Scripture reminds us, is at the root of all evil. Gavin Blackwell, not unlike many who have come before him, and, no doubt, will come after, learned that lesson the hard way. Perhaps it is a lesson that all of us should be continually reminded of.

Joe returned to school the following week, trying to regain some semblance of a normal life. Everyone was still very excited about all the events of the previous week. Joe tried to accommodate everyone who would ask him questions and attempt to get his reaction to everything that had happened, including the news media who couldn't get enough of the story.

One afternoon, he was finally able to steal away for a few minutes during his recreation period. He headed upstairs in Moreau Hall to pay a visit to the chapel, hoping to find some quiet time. Fortunately, this part of the building still remained open while other parts were closed for cleanup and restoration from the damage incurred during the break-in.

He entered the chapel, knelt down, and began to pray. *"Bonjour,* my son," came a familiar greeting from the back of the chapel. Startled at first, thinking he was alone, Joe quickly turned to see Father Simon seated behind him.

"Father, it's good to see you."

"And you as well, *mon ami."*

"I have come to the chapel today to give thanks for all that has happened to our school, including my thanks to you," explained Joe.

"Tres bien! Dieu est bon! God is good!" replied Father as he smiled. "It is the Lord who provides for us. We are merely the instruments of His will.

"My son," he continued, "there has been much good accomplished here these past few days. I come today to encourage you to continue in the work that lies ahead. The gracious gift that was bestowed upon your school, though greatly needed, will only last so long. In the end, it is not money that continues to sustain this school and others like it, but the grace of God. In the Gospel, Our Lord encourages us not to worry about the things we need. Our heavenly Father knows what we need and will provide them for us. Instead, we should seek first to building the Kingdom of God, and everything we need will be given to us.

"The true work of the Church requires people who are dedicated to the work of building God's kingdom here on earth. I ask you, in particular, my son, to answer to the Lord's call in whatever vocation he calls you to in helping to build that Kingdom. As the Gospel reminds us, 'the harvest is abundant, but the workers are few.' And, as it further states, all we need do is 'ask the Master of the harvest to send out workers for His harvest.' Let us continue to work and pray toward that end.

"I leave you with this, *mon ami*. Continue to walk in the Lord and be a beacon of His light to others. I am always available to you in moments of prayer. Although I leave you now, you will see me again very soon in the company of another.

"*Au revoir*, my son, and God bless you!"

Joe bowed his head and crossed himself as Father extended his blessing. When Joe looked up, Father Simon was gone.

It was getting well into the evening by the time Joe was able to leave school. Baseball practice had gone a little longer, and he had helped break down the stage set in the auditorium after a very successful weekend run of *Les Mis*, including a final performance that literally went out with a bang!

He walked out the front entrance of the school, looking to see if his dad's car was approaching yet. Not seeing it, he looked to his left and saw a light shining from the top of Moreau Hall. It was not a normal light but another kind of light that he had come to recognize. He walked closer and could see the Roman soldier standing atop the tower, his hand extended as one offering a greeting or to bid farewell. Suddenly, he heard the voice of the soldier in his head, as in an interior locution, saying to him, "Well done, my good and faithful servant, for the Master rejoices in you.

Continue His work, fight the good fight of faith, and go in the peace and the love of God. To the King be honor and glory!"

Joe turned as his dad's car suddenly pulled up beside him. He turned back to look above Moreau Hall, but the light was no longer there.

~~~~~

In the days that followed, life slowly began to return to normal in the Pryce family. There were only a few more weeks left before the end of the school year and the beginning of summer break. All the excitement surrounding the dramatic events of the past couple of weeks was gradually subsiding. At least, that's what everyone thought.

The house phone was ringing, but no one seemed to be able to pick it up. It finally stopped. Almost immediately, it began ringing again. Mr. Pryce, who had been toiling at his workbench in the garage, came in through the kitchen door. "Can't somebody answer the phone?" he called out. "Hello," he said into the phone receiver as he finally picked it up. Joe was upstairs in his room studying for a major history test scheduled for tomorrow in Mr. McAuliffe's class. "Joe!" he heard his dad calling from downstairs. "Joe! I need you in the kitchen, quickly!"

Joe rushed down the steps. By the sound of his dad's voice, it sounded urgent. He hurried into the kitchen and found his dad standing with the phone in his hand and a stunned look on his face. "Son," he began, "you're not going to believe this, but the White House is on the line and wants to speak with you!"

"Yeah, right," answered Joe. "Look, Dad, I've got homework I'm in the middle of. Can ya stop it with the pranks?"

"This is no joke, son. Here, take the phone before they hang up. I'm sure they've got plenty of other things they're doing." Suddenly his dad had a serious look on his face suggesting that maybe this wasn't a joke after all. He took the phone from his dad. Mr. Pryce then left the kitchen to give Joe some privacy.

"Hello?" said Joe somewhat feebly.

"Is this Joe?" a woman's voice asked very politely.

"Yes, ma'am," answered Joe, trying to clear his throat.

"Please hold for the president," she informed him. After a short pause, Joe then heard a series of clicks followed by a voice he recognized from having heard it on the television, the radio, or the internet, but never over the phone, until now.

"Joe?" a distinctive and enthusiastic voice said through the phone.

"Yes, sir," answered Joe, not quite knowing what else to say.

"It's a real pleasure to finally have a chance to speak with you," the voice said.

"Uh, thank you, sir, uh, the pleasure is all mine," responded Joe, still struggling to find his voice. It sure sounded like the president, he thought to himself.

"Joe, I've been reading the papers and watching on television all about the wonderful thing you did for your school a couple of weeks ago."

"Thank you, sir," responded Joe.

"To be honest," continued the president, "I was even more impressed with how you attributed much of what happened to the strong faith of your school community and especially to the intercession of a number of saints, did I hear right?" he asked.

"Well, yes sir, Mr. President," responded Joe, his voice finally returning, "we have much to be thankful for. Prayer can be a very powerful thing, and we have many advocates in heaven who are there to help us." Joe was suddenly feeling a bit more at ease.

"You are absolutely right about that, Joe!" responded the president. "In fact, I have a number of favorite saints I like to rely on myself." He paused for a moment. "And that goes directly, at least in part, to the reason why I'm calling. I would like to invite you and your family to a weekend stay with my family and me at

Camp David in Maryland sometime soon. Perhaps, when we are finished speaking here tonight, you can put your dad back on the line, and I will have him speak to someone here to arrange a date."

"Really? That would be great!" answered Joe.

"By the way," continued the president, "I understand you enjoy mountain biking, is that right?"

"Yes, I do, Mr. President, very much," replied Joe.

"Terrific! I invite you to bring your bike and join me on a ride through some great trails I know up there. There is one in particular that leads very close to one of my favorite places in the area—the Grotto of Our Lady of Lourdes."

"Yes, I've been there myself," said Joe.

"So I've been told," replied the president. "There is someone of particular importance to me who is often there, an old priest friend of mine whom I believe is a mutual acquaintance of ours. I am hoping to have the opportunity to see him again there and would very much like for you to come along with me. What do you say?"

"I am honored to accept, Mr. President, and very much look forward to it."

"So do I, Joe, so do I! Until then, good night, Joe, and God bless you!"

"Thank you, Mr. President, and God bless you too!"

Made in the USA
Lexington, KY
12 August 2018